# THEY PREFER IT HIDDEN

Published by Kenneth Falb

# ACKNOWLEDGEMENTS

**To those who contributed their labor in getting this novel published:**

Thank you to Matthew Crane and Brandon Wheeler in providing advice as beta readers for the book.

Thank you Driss Chaoui for designing and illustrating the novel's cover.

Thank you George Jreije for providing their skills in editing.


**Special thanks to those who supported me in my writing and publishing process:**

Thank you to my love Adrianna Hargrove for supporting me all throughout my writing process.

This book is made in honor of my dad. You were excited

to hear I was making one, and I hope you would have

loved it all the same reading it.

# TABLE OF CONTENTS

# CHAPTER 1

I'm Jonathan Whitlock, the resident occult investigator for the humble town of Helford. Saying I've seen things is a bit of an understatement. There's always new lessons to learn in this job, mainly ones about not dying. As it turns out I'm pretty good at that. Most wouldn't call what I do fun, but that's because it's an acquired taste. I've had to contend with a lot while stuck in the jaws of a rabid leprechaun. It's a road full of speed bumps, all originating from one man, my uncle.

Uncle Whitty was an interesting individual. He was the kind of guy to find whimsy at breakfast and magic at dinner. He'd point to a circle of mushrooms and tell me faeries made them. When visiting his home in Helford, he'd take out his telescope and show me the constellations.

One strange memory I have is about how he acted about the basement. I was nine, messing with one of my coloring books on the living room carpet. Drawing didn't seem to cure my boredom, so I got up and wandered. Most of the house was open to me, but the basement stairs caught my eye over everything else. Judging it from a child's eye, the basement was a dark place people rarely ever went to.

Most times it was drowned out by silence, but this time, a light melodic hum came deep from its concrete lungs. It beckoned me to go further down, the sound too familiar to be unfriendly. I did as it asked. Each step I took was even and unafraid.

Inside the basement, I stopped at a massive wood door. It was dark and smooth to the touch, resembling obsidian in the dimly lit room. Etched into it were scenes of deep forests. Overlooking this other world was a man whose beard melded with the forests beneath him.

The hum was now in my ear. At that moment, it felt like the most important thing in the world. I reached for the door handle. Before I could pull it, Uncle Whitty appeared and snatched me away from it. He held onto me tight, his breath tinged with panic and exhaustion.

"Not him damn it… anything but him," he said to the door.

Knelt down to my level, Uncle Whitty said "Johnny, you need to listen to me carefully. I know you're smart, but some things are too dangerous for our own good. Don't be touching nothing down here, okay?"

I gave a confused nod, and he hugged me again.

Even after all those years being away from him, it was hard to shake the realness of that moment. Whatever doubts I gained growing up would always have to contend with that feeling.

He didn't talk to a lot of people, at least that's what the rest of my family said of him. His home was a ways out of town, the pristine isolation feeling straight out of a murder mystery. Whenever I visited for the night as a kid, I could swear I heard an organ playing.

That was the kind of atmosphere he brought. It was something the rest of my family found too eccentric. My family one day stopped talking about him. It was like someone flipped a switch and they all forgot about him. Once I was the age to ask why, he had already become a distant memory.

All this to say, I was not expecting to get anything from his inheritance. I couldn't even go to his funeral since my landlord was having me evicted by then.

I wasn't special growing up. I didn't do clubs, sports, or really anything. School wasn't my strong suit either. I was in the middle of the road. Those things don't matter at the time, but you start feeling it later on. It matters in an emotional sense. I became an adult waiting for the real fun to begin, for people to pop out the bushes and tell me that none of the stuff before needed to matter. Technically it didn't matter, but more so in the way that the stuff you worked hard on was useless in college. Adulthood was more responsibilities arriving too soon.

Now at the age of twenty-two, I fell asleep on my naked mattress with the calming metronome of water drops on my forehead. I paid a thousand a month for a one bedroom apartment with a landlord who refused to fix anything. Jobs were hard to come by, both from scarcity and a lack of passion. It wasn't that I couldn't imagine what I wanted to do. I wanted to explore the world, smell leaves, and feel dirt between my fingers. The issue was those aren't entry jobs, and those were the ones that were always available. They call them dream jobs for a reason. Besides, they were for the people I thought I wasn't. Every day, I was one text away from going back to live with my parents.

The day of my eviction, I was stacking boxes shoulder high and praying they wouldn't collapse on me later. The funeral had passed a day or so ago. By then, I had sent all the condolences I could to my grandparents, which most of my family neglected to do.

I was just about to be ready to load my car, when I heard a knock at the door. When I answered, I was shocked to find no one there, nothing except a letter. Underneath that was a box. Bringing the letter with me inside, I sat down at my dinner table and opened it. It was chock full of legalese and statements. What caught my eye was a section called "STATEMENT".

It read, "Johnny Boy, if you're reading this, you know what happened to me. I had a lot of responsibilities, and I know damn well someone needs to take them over after I croak. The rest of the family isn't made for it, but you are. I'm giving you the house. Whatever's in it is yours too. I kept the telescope, just in case you wanna check on me. Wherever you are and whatever you're planning, make sure to do it better than I did."

It took me a second to process the letter. The air felt freer, and the grass outside got greener. For the first time in my life, I owned a house. My mind had a field day coming up with new things to be anxious about. There was a silver lining. I wouldn't have to move back in with my parents.

# CHAPTER 2

Helford could be anywhere in the US. It's smiling faces at a bakery that smells of gingerbread. A downtown filled with quaint brick buildings which have lasted since antebellum. Suburban neighborhoods with HOAs that hate the word "change." Everyone is bored from sterilized living, their only escape being to judge others less fortunate. If you grew up there, you wanted to leave. If you didn't, you couldn't afford to live there anyway. Before my uncle's death, I only ever visited Helford a few times.

Coming up to my uncle's house felt like unlocking an old memory. Driving up the gravel driveway, sticks crunching under my wheels. Fall had arrived. Red and orange leaves sloped down shingles as black as infected wood. Triangle windows, more gothic cathedral than quaint home, pointed to the heavens. The house was defiant, the forest circling it like wolves. Seeing it again made me realize my uncle had the dramatic flair of a vampire.

Getting out, the first thing I pulled out was the box that was left at my door. I hadn't opened it. Knowing my uncle, he would have wanted it that way. Twisting the handle, the door creaked open. Further in, I discovered a home long lost.

Furniture drowned in dust and grime. It was so thick it could be wiped off like snow on porch railing. Stairs groaned under me, the upper floors tasting of mildew. I dragged my fingers on the leaf pattern walls, a fine layer of dust collecting on my fingertips.

At the end of the second floor was the first guest room, which was where I always slept. Entering it, I was shocked to find it maintained better than the rest of the house. The desk and floor were clean. Inside the drawers were the old fantasy stories I wrote as a kid. Each story was given its own binder, the lined paper inside now laminated.

I felt like a giant sitting on my bed. The sheets were soft. Race cars sped around the clean edges of my comforters.

The bookshelf still had the books Uncle Whitty got me. The classics were higher up where Uncle Whitty could reach. The rare fantasy book was placed closer down to the eye level of the bed. It was the same as when I had left it. The same as he would want me to see it.

Seeing the other rooms further hammered in how different my room was. Trash filled my uncle's office and dirty clothes piled in his bedroom. Some rooms were blocked off with storage boxes and random bits and bobs. Seeing this made me wonder about my uncle. Did he become a hoarder as he became more distant from everything, or was it just always a part of him that I had never noticed?

I noticed something strange about each box. Some boxes were normal, and unmarked, while others had strange symbols drawn into them with red sharpie.

Trying to lift one of the marked boxes, I accidentally dropped a wooden case that was on top of it. Hitting the ground, the case popped open to reveal a revolver. The gun misfired, the shot hitting me square in the forehead.

"Ow!" I yelped, feeling a welt form on my head.

The bullet fell straight down and rolled across the wooden floor. It looked like a real bullet but hit me with all the force of a metal pellet.

I picked up the gun, aiming it at the wall.

"Huh, Uncle Whitty never told me anything about owning a toy gun," I said.

I pulled the trigger, wanting to test the supposed pellet gun on the worn walls. Instead, the thing fired with the same kick back of an actual gun. Having not braced myself, the gun's barrel smacked against my chin. The bullet went straight through the wall in front of me along with the wall after that. Once my wide eyes had settled, I tucked the gun and its case back where I found it.

Processing all this made me dizzy. Each disorganized pile begged to be cleaned. Each piece of junk gave me one more thing I needed to do. I was frustrated with both myself and my uncle. All this time, all this isolation. He had transformed his house and maybe even himself into something unrecognizable, yet a part of him still hoped to see me again.

Stumbling down the trash covered stairs, I tried to decompress at the table in the kitchen. My fingers tapped the box, still unopened. Curiosity was getting the best of me, and I couldn't think of any better time to see what was inside. Peeling off the tape revealed a leather bound journal. Embroidered on the cover was a snake moving in a square-like pattern. The snake's fang resembled an ancient Arthurian dagger.

Written on the book's side was the phrase "Danger hides under blades."

My uncle was a crazy guy, but even this was too much. Skimming through the journal, I saw strange sketches and descriptions. They described things straight out of a fantasy book. It told of nature-like fae that stole children in the dead of night, and human-like parasites who fed off the social discomfort of people around them. The drawings were just short of esoteric pencil scratches. He made it for me, which made the book a few pounds heavier. The last piece of Uncle Whitty I would ever experience for the first time. From now on, I would be digging at memories to find him. Thinking more about it left a gross aftertaste.

Those thoughts were forced on hold when the doorbell hummed a cheerful tune. At the door was a woman thirty or so years my senior. When I opened the door, she seemed confused that I was the one answering.

We both said hello and she asked, "Is Mr. Whitlock home?"

"Oh, well… He passed away just a few days ago."

"Oh my goodness," she said, "I'm so sorry to bother you. If you want me to, I'll just get going."

She was just about to leave when I said "Wait."

I didn't know exactly why I said that. I wanted questions answered and I didn't know where to look, and she was the closest person to ask. I looked for something to say.

"What were you seeing him for?" I asked.

"He was going to help me with a certain… situation. Yeah, situation," she said,

Hearing that only made me want to ask more questions.

"It'd be rude if I didn't get you something warm to drink before you left. After all, we're so out of the way," I said, adding, "besides, he's my uncle, and as long as it isn't computer trouble, I can help too."

With it being so chilly outside, the woman accepted my offer. I guided her over to the kitchen, the second cleanest part of the house. That's when I got her name, Mrs. Seer. She sat at the dining table while I set up some tea.

I was looking for the kettle when she asked, "So you're his nephew?"

"Yeah, is that shocking?" I said.

"Not a lot of people knew your uncle, so anything about him is surprising," Mrs. Seer answered.

"Did he not talk to a lot of people?" I asked.

"Not exactly, the opposite really. He helped a lot of people. In fact, he was an important figure in Helford, so important people never asked him about things he wouldn't want to answer," she said.

"Hm, I couldn't imagine someone being that important," I said.

"You'd be surprised," she said.

I was looking for a way to respond when I found the kettle, stocked neatly by the dust bunnies.

"Any preference on tea?" I asked.

"What do you have?" Mrs. Seer asked.

"From the looks of it, all of the teas," I said.

She pondered. "I'll take jasmine."

Bringing the jasmine tea down, I saw Mrs. Seer eying the journal my uncle left me.
Giving it a look over, she asked "Do you know what your uncle… did?"

"No," I blurted. Realizing what I had said, I cleared my throat and said, "No, I didn't. Do you?"
She looked away from me, playing with her hands. "I do. I'm just worried it'll be confusing for a non-Helfordian."

I sat down in front of her "Mrs. Seer, I'd really appreciate knowing more about my uncle. I have time to understand."

Mrs. Seer looked down at her hands, then back at me. "People in Helford want one thing more than anything, and that's normalcy. We want people to think we are as well put together as anyone else. Yet the world doesn't actually work that way. Helford's brimming with things beyond the norm. They're wild, strange, and difficult for just about anyone to really hold down and control. That's what your uncle did. He kept the weird under wraps so we could keep acting like we were normal. It's why I came here. I needed help dealing with the weird."

I leaned against my chair, thinking. She was right, this was beyond anything I thought my uncle did. It felt like a joke, like she'd burst out laughing any second, but she never did. It made me think more about the house. What was my uncle hiding in here? The more I thought, the more I wanted to put my mind to something else.

"What was the help you needed?" I said.

She seemed hesitant to tell me more, but said, "It was about my son. After he got fired from his work, he went off the deep end. Every night, he's been doing strange rituals. I'm really scared about what he might do next. What if he hurts himself? I just don't know how to help him."

A second went by with both of us in total silence, only interrupted by the screaming kettle. I got up and poured both of us a cup of tea. I took a sip of mine, weighing my decisions. I had no idea what was going on, and I couldn't tell whether helping would make the situation worse. Yet, every time I thought of telling her no, a mountain of boxes and trash filled my mind.

"I'll do it," I said.

"Wait, really?" she said, surprised. I don't blame her, I was too.

I was feeling too confident for my own good.

"Are you sure? I don't want you to get hurt doing something that isn't your responsibility," she said.

I traded looks between the journal and her, and said, "I can't say a lot about myself, but one thing I can say is that I know how to jump into something and learn as I go." Leaning in, I said, "Just give me a time and place and I'll be there."

Once we finished tea, I guided Mrs. Seer back to her car. She thanked me and drove off down the gravel road, autumn leaves following fast behind. I waited till her car was gone to go to my car and start unloading my stuff.

I had very little, the unpacking taking less than an hour. For now, I kept my boxes in the kitchen to organize later. I planned on putting my stuff away when I already had my uncle's house clean and in order. It'd be a while before that happened.

With my boxes in the kitchen, I dusted off a chair and began to read the journal. I had only a few hours before I would jump headfirst into something totally out of my element. If this was really what my uncle had planned for me, I sure hoped he knew what he was talking about.

# CHAPTER 3

Coming up to Mrs. Seer's house, the first thing I noticed was the smoke curling from her backyard. It was still light out the sun just starting to set. From the little I could read, occult rituals were tedious to the point that only crazy people were willing to go that extra mile.

Everyone was still going on with their day. Children played football two front yards over. A man across the street was coming back from work. All the while, loud chanting droned on from Mrs. Seer's backyard.

Wasting no more time, I went to the door and knocked. Mrs. Seer answered, waving me into the house. We took a short walk into the living room. A TV played old game shows. Food trays were set up by the sofa, a dog begging beside it. Mrs. Seer went over to the screen door, sliding it open.

"You ready?" she said.

"As much as I can be," I said, giving the dog a few pats on the head.

I walked out with Mrs. Seer. Before me was an above ground pool at the corner of the yard, and at the center a fire pit. At the pit was a bonfire, tall, in the shape of a tent. Orbiting the fire was Mrs. Seer's son. Dressed in a black robe and deer antlers taped on a scooter helmet, he swung a wooden staff any way he could.

He looked to be the same age as me, which made this a bit awkward. From the way the mom was describing this, I was expecting less man-child and more actual child. Underneath the robe was an oversized sleep shirt accentuated by a worker's tan. Long, somewhat curled brunette hair streamed down a freckled face. He was unhinged, but he wasn't bad looking at all.

"By the name of Hermes Trismegistus, by the Sorcerers of Prague, and all spirits who heed my call! Unite and obey my bidding for I am Tomas Bellll…" His words trailed off the second he noticed us watching.

"Thomas, we have a visitor," Mrs. Seer said.

"*Mom*, my name's not Thomas, it's Tomas," her son said.

"I thought that was your ritual name," she responded.

"I'm mid-ritual, mom. And who is he?" Tomas asked.

"I'm Johnathan Whitlock. Your mom called me here to stop you," I said.

Tomas shot a look between his mom and me, ending at his mom.

"Mom!" Tomas whined.

"Honey, I had to. You're trying to end the world," she said.

Hearing that, I swung my head to Mrs. Seer. "You didn't tell me that."

"No! I'm ending twenty percent of it, give or take. The bad stuff mostly," Tomas said to his mom.

"Doesn't matter what amount. I'm going to have to stop you," I responded.

"Great. If anyone feels hungry, just holler and I'll order a pizza," Mrs. Seer said, closing the screen door on her way inside.

Looking from the door to me, Tomas crossed his arms and said, "Whatever you got planned, it's not going to work."

"Are we going to have to fight?" I asked Tomas.

"What? No, I bruise easily." Tomas recoiled.

"I'm not leaving till you stop this ridiculousness," I said, walking towards the bonfire.

Tomas hid behind the fire, yelling, "No way, I'm waving this stick till my ritual is complete!"

"Give me that," I said, running around to try to grab the stick.

An embarrassing amount of time passed as I chased Tomas all around the bonfire. At the end of it, Tomas ran to the pool's patio. He swung the gate closed, smacking my hands whenever I would try to get close. I had never been in a fight, and I didn't have a weapon to make up for it. I backed away, my patience running thin.

"Get down here this instant," I said.

"What are you? My dad? I'm not doing that," Tomas said.

"Maybe if you started acting like an adult, I'd start talking to you like one," I bit back.

"Well unlike you, I've got enough going on with me not to get into other people's business," he said.

It went like that for a while. Soon the sun began to set, the sky settling into soft oranges and purples. The fire stayed strong. A few times it started weakening, but Tomas pestered me into adding more wood to it. As time passed by, I got a lawn chair to sit in. Boredom started to settle in for both of us.

"So this is it huh? My BBEG is some guy lighting fires in his backyard."

"Your what?" Tomas asked.

"Big Bad Evil Guy, it's a story thing… well a roleplaying thing," I explained.

"Isn't roleplaying a sex thing?" Tomas questioned.

"Wha—no," I stammered back.

We went silent again.

"I'm not an evil guy. I just—I just don't like bad things," Tomas said, now laying on the patio.

"Bad how?" I asked.

"You know, like war, disease, people who leave their carts out instead of putting them in cart return, health insurance companies."

"Seems a bit diverse in terms of awfulness," I said.

"Hey, if you can get rid of one of those things, why not get rid of all those things?" Tomas said.

"Can't argue with that. Hard to imagine a spell being able to do all that though."

I leaned against my chair. Resting my eyes, I was knocked awake when a book was tossed square onto my lap. Being hardcover, it stung. "Liber Perverso Magic," the cover said in gold lettering.

"Page ninety-nine, read it and weep." Noticing the confused look on my face, he said, "Go ahead. I memorized the whole book already."

Flipping through the pages, I saw passage after passage of spell instructions. The format resembled a cookbook, a huge chunk of each section being the writer telling their life story with little of it actually being about the spell. Then a small guide was made with spell ingredients and steps to execute it. With a bit of turning, I made it to the world-ending spell Tomas was using.

The ingredients were as follows:

*One dried newt*

*Five sheep knuckles*

*A cup of ash*

The instructions then said:

*Mix all ingredients mentioned*

*Start a massive fire, chant incantation until fire turns apple green, start over if it is emerald green*

*Once green, add mixture and say final lines of incantation*

*Close eyes and concentrate, now you have your very own apocalypse*

I stared at the instructions. I read them a second and then a third time. I even read them sideways. I then realized something that changed everything.

"Alright, you can come out now," I said.

"Wait… really?" Tomas said, puzzled.

"You changed my mind, I'll help you," I said, getting up from my chair. "I'll pick up a pizza and get us some beers to celebrate after the spell."

"I—I can't believe it." Tomas ran down excitedly. "What convinced you?"

"You're right, the world sucks and it would be nice to make it better," I said.

"Glad to have you on the team. Now nothing can stop me."

Tomas rose his staff in victory.

"I'll hurry up so I can see the fireworks."

The ritual went back into motion. The bonfire's flames changed from orange to green. Two pizzas and a bag of breadsticks sat at the garden table. I stayed on my lawn chair, a twelve pack beside me. I watched the light show, Tomas dancing around it like a cheerleader from hell. The green flame grew bigger and bigger, eclipsing the logs that kept it. It turned into a twisting pillar of flame. The inferno was so tall that I needed to crane my neck to see the top.

The moment came, when the fire turned the color of a ripe granny smith. Seeing this, Tomas smiled like a kid at Disneyland. He grabbed his bag, pouring the ingredients straight into the fire. The fire somehow grew even bigger, and Tomas had to take some steps away not to get burned.

"The time has come, ring those trumpets and sing. Sing!" Tomas chanted.

Tomas closed his eyes, entering a meditative state. The flames dissipated. No grand explosion, no angel cries, nothing. They went away with the fanfare of a whimper. Tomas opened his eyes, looking around shocked and confused.

"Wha—What happened? Did it work?" He ran over to the book, flipping to the right page. He started to pant, his eyes glossy. "I did everything it said, swear I did. What did I do wrong? What did I—"

"Thomas! Stop that racket or I'm calling the sheriff!" An old neighbor a house over yelled.

Tomas ignored the neighbor. "I—I don't understand."

"Are you listening? Or did all this bumming around make you forget how to—"

"I said I'm done!" Tomas interrupted.

The two went silent, the neighbor slamming his window soon after. I looked back and forth, my arm just about to reach for a beer.

"What did you do?" Tomas whispered.

I didn't hear him, and said, "What did you say?"

He stomped over to me, grabbing me by the nape. He seethed, "What did you do? How did you stop it?"

"I didn't do anything," I said.

"Then what went wrong?" His voice rose.

"The ingredients were too easy to get. Anyone could do that spell. No way that spell existed over a thousand years and no one tried it at least once," I explained.

"So... it couldn't ever work," he whimpered, letting me go.

"Not in a million years," I said.

Tomas wandered about the backyard, his arms dragging behind him. Sitting down on the grass, he stared at the ground. I got up and sat in front of him. He looked up, listless.

I offered him a beer and said, "I'll get ya a slice."

Three beers in, we sat together rambling at the garden table. While I was three in, Tomas was already far gone by one. He slurred each word, his face flat on the cold metal of the table. Our bellies were full of cheese, bread, and marinara.

"You know, I love mah mom. I love her very much," Tomas said.

"Mhm," I responded.

"But… I just can't be living with her, you know?" he said.

"I feel ya," I said.

"Like, I'm twenty-two, that's like twenty twos. It's too much… but I can't," he grumbled.

I looked over to him and asked, "Why not?"

"'Cause all of… you know. Jobs sucks, pay bad. And when I need the time to find something good for me, I just remember my mom will need to foot the bill." Tomas went silent "It sucks. Sucks real hard."

I held a can of beer, the darkness obscuring the bottom. Bugs buzzed near my ear.

What Tomas said was all too familiar to me. I struggled so hard to leave my parents' home and feel like I had just a bit of control on my life. What I found instead were days filled with constant fear and isolation. I still can't say what kind of choice moving out was. Things would always be hard, but at least now I was out and able to make my own choices. Inheriting a house, even if it's full of garbage, was still a godsend for anyone.

"You can live with me," I muttered.

"What?" Tomas said, lifting his head from the table.

"It's not in great shape. But if we start working on it, we'll have something really good on our hands." I took a sip from my drink. "Just keep the sink empty, respect my uncle's stuff, and you can stay as long as you like."

"But…" Tomas said. "But why?"

"You think I know? House is too empty… need someone to talk to," I said.

"Oh." Tomas went quiet, a soft smile appearing on his face. "Thanks."

"No problem," I said.

With Tomas's help, cleaning was going a lot easier than I expected. We swept the stairs, dusted the shelves, cleaned garbage off the floors, and reorganized almost everything in the house. Tomas chose the second guest bedroom. I stayed in my old room. I wasn't ready to stay in my uncle's room just yet.

Hacking down the clutter jungle, we had cleared every single box that my uncle hoarded. We kept what we liked and threw away or donated what we could do without. It was beginning to look like a livable house, though the house was now more barebones, as we had thrown out most of the furniture because of mold.

One day, Mrs. Seer came to visit. Before she left, she gave me a few hundred dollars. She said she wanted to pay me the same amount my uncle was paid doing the work he did. Feeling that wad of cash made me realize I may have a good gig going with all this supernatural stuff.

After four weeks, we had one group of boxes left: the ones marked as being occult. Looking over them, I decided to trust my uncle and not open them. Cursed or not, I wasn't going to risk finding a monkey's paw. To keep the house clear, we stored all the mystery boxes in the basement. Every few days or so, I would go down to check on them. I stopped checking up on them after the first few times. That one door made me too uneasy. Every time I'd get near the thing, it would start rattling.

# CHAPTER 4

I'd never been in a mayor's office before, but I
expected it to be a lot bigger. Instead it was the same size as
the five other offices we had to pass to get there. What
separated the mayor's office from the rest was the desk.
The thing was heavier than a granite slab and stretched
from one side of the room to the other. Its reflection put
mirrors to shame, giving only a slight tint of lacquered
mahogany.

Showing up earlier than expected, we waited while
the mayor dealt with other issues. I sat still, hands clasped.
Tomas, on the other hand, played with the desk's
paperweights.

Tomas had felt antsy after a month of doing nothing
at my uncle's house. He'd been unemployed the whole

time, still struggling to link the passions he had in magic with a steady income. By the time I'd gotten the call from the mayor, he had already used every coloring book and jigsaw puzzle in the house. I didn't see a problem with him coming. I had no idea what I was doing either way.

"Dude, this is so cool. On your second mission, and you're already getting calls from politicians." Tomas pointed over to one of the mayor's decorations. "She even has a holographic clock."

Mayor Harriet Maelie opened her office door, and said, "Oh great, you're on time. Good sign."

Hearing her voice, Tomas scrambled to place the paperweight back where it was. In one motion, he placed it on the table, clasped his hands and straightened his back. He moved his head around, nodding in a way that was supposed to be unassuming. Harriet Maelie tilted her head but continued like it never happened.

From the little Tomas had told me, Harriet Maelie was a piece of mayoral royalty. Her family kept a tight grip on Helford's politics. For as long as people could remember, if someone needed strings pulled, they would ask for a Maelie. That ability to make things happen had made them both heroes and villains to the people in the town. Harriet was the newest Maelie on the block, and thus unproven. Because of that, Helford had yet to form an opinion about her.

Harriet shook my hand and said, "It's nice to meet you Mr. Whitlock. My father had amazing things to say about your uncle."

"Thank you, I hope you'll feel the same about me," I said.

"I'm sure I will." Harriet then turned to Tomas. "And you're?"

"Thomas Seer. I'm his new partner," Tomas said.

"I thought your name was Tomas?" I whispered.

"I don't know her like that," he whispered.

"Alright, let's see," Harriet said under her breath.

Her desk went from wall to wall, and she needed to get to the other side. She shimmied around us.

"Excuse me, pardon me… sorry. Yep, wuh—oh. There we go."

Sliding over the top of her desk, she managed to get to the other side, though not without knocking over a few pens and paper.

Harriet sighed. "Okay, now let's talk about your job."

"I'm listening," I said, leaning forward.

"Things have been going fine… but that's sort of the issue. It's fine but not great. I need something good to stay in office, and that's where you'll come in."

Opening one of her drawers, Harriet dropped an old gray photo in front of us. The photo was of a forest, at the center of it a figure. Its eyes glowed from the camera flash, two whites piercing the dark. Even with its hunched stature, the creature towered high. It had to be at least seven feet.

"This is Basket Case," Harriet said.

"The heck is she?" I asked.

"Ever heard of basket women? Those monsters meant to scare kids into behaving? Well, turns out they're more than just stories," Harriet said.

"Oh yeah, my grandma told me about her. Freaky," Tomas said.

Eying the creature, I realized Uncle Whitty may have warned me about it too. He always did tell me to not go into the forests alone.

"What do you know about Basket Case?" I asked.

Harriet grabbed one of her dropped pens, clicking it. "Apart from her victims, not much. We sort of relegated that responsibility to your uncle. Basket Case kidnapped children. At first she did so in the forests, but something caused her to move deeper into the town."

"What happened to the kids?" I asked.

"I was always told she eats them," Tomas remarked.

"You'd think, but it's actually even more strange. We—well your uncle mostly— would find the kids totally feral. Takes months to help them to readjust," Harriet said.

I leaned back, pressing my finger against my lip, and nodding. "I see. You want me to take care of Basket Case."

Harriet looked at me confused.

"What? No." She gave a lukewarm smile. "You have me mistaken. I don't want you to get at Basket Case. Not even your uncle could do that."

"Oh. What, uh… what do you want me to do?" I asked.

"My family has dealt with Basket Case for a very long time, and we've come up with our own system. Whenever elections were close, maybe a year or so in advance, we'd send your uncle down to Basket Case's lair, where he'd then save a few children from her gnarly little fingers. Makes for great photoshoots," Harriet explained.

"Aren't you just repeating the same problem over and over again?" I said.

"People need problems, Mr. Whitlock. It's what brings them to the polls. My brother, when he was mayor, didn't do the same. And what happened to him? He didn't end up reelected."

Tomas spoke up, "I thought he wasn't reelected because of 'The Incident'."

"The whatcident?" I said.

"We don't talk about 'The Incident,'" Harriet got up from her desk and walked to the window, opening the blinds to reveal a brick wall. "Either way, I need those children rescued. Otherwise people will think I did nothing as Mayor."

While Harriet stared out the window, Tomas and I shot a look at each other.

"She really didn't," Tomas mouthed to me.

Harriet turned around and asked us, "So, what'll be your price?"

At deeper viewing, there was little going for Harriet Maelie. If she got reelected Mayor, at best, a few park benches would get set up. I couldn't with good conscience say yes to perpetuating this, but I also couldn't blow her off. She was still the Mayor. All there was to do now was highball and hope she wouldn't want to pay.

"Hmmm. I'd be risking a lot to do this, so it can't be cheap. Ten grand is my starting price," I said, grabbing two pieces of gum from my pocket for Tomas and me.

"Alright, I can do that," she said,

I almost swallowed the gum I was chewing on.

"Really?" I exclaimed.

"I mean, yeah, you are professional occult investigators right?" Harriet said.

Tomas and I traded looks.

"Make it twelve grand," I said.

"Done."

"Woo, hot tub here we come," Tomas said.

"I don't think you know how much a hot tub costs," I said.

"Not with that attitude," Tomas said back.

"I'll send a quarter of the payment up front and the rest after you do the job. A pleasure doing business," Harriet said, again shaking our hands.

Eying that paycheck up and down, it made a bit more sense why Uncle Whitty would stoop to do Maelie's dirty work. We left the moment we got the chance, both to prepare and to freak out over our first big job without Maelie seeing us.

# CHAPTER 5

If I was a basket woman and wanted to kidnap children, the first place I'd look is a playground. That's the best explanation I can give for us staking out a children's playground late at night.

We were close to downtown, right beside the outside sculpture called "Garbage Day." Describing Garbage Day would be a disservice to it. All I can say is I never imagined a melted plastic man could make me feel so melancholic.

Wood chips padded the area, the kind that get lost in shoe soles. The seesaw and the slides stood still, colored a deep green. Street lights saturated the sidewalks and basketball court. Deep shadows projected down the chain link fence.

We watched from afar in the parking lot, using binoculars my uncle stored away for birdwatching. It must have been a short hobby, since they were in mint condition. Tomas and I sat in my beat up Corolla, eating donuts we got as a stakeout snack.

"So, with Basket Case, what's the plan when we see her?" Tomas asked.

"My uncle did write a bit about her. He says that if you place a creepy looking doll around, she'll get distracted by it long enough for us to snag a few kids to safety," I responded.

"You saying she brings a purse full of kids? Like she's running errands?" Tomas asked.

"Yep, so that's the safest way to rescue a few feral kids. The dangerous way is following her and finding her current lair," I said.

Tomas wiped his hands of sprinkles. "Sure hope you got some defenses for if she finds us."

"Do you?" I said.

"Uh huh, check it." Tomas pulled out an electric shaver. Tapping the button, Tomas's hand began vibrating with the shaver. I was not impressed.

"What are you planning to do with that?" I asked.

"That's a surprise," Tomas said.

"Then my thing will be a surprise when we get the doll," I said back.

Tomas let out a small "Aw," as he turned off the shaver.

"While we're waiting, tell me about 'The Incident,' the one about Harriet's brother," I said.

"I don't know why. It's got nothing to do with this," Tomas said.

"It's not really crazy to be curious about stuff like that," I said, looking through my binoculars.

"I guess. People in Helford aren't really about asking questions like that."

Percival Maelie, Harriet's brother, had to step down as Mayor of Helford over an incident which nearly tainted his entire family. It's something people only talk about in whispers behind veils thicker than tar.

Despite being a blue-blooded member of the established Maelie dynasty, Percival was a fresh start compared to his ancient father. Having received a blank check from his family, Percival was guaranteed to win.

Things were great at the start. In a town where stasis was the norm, Percival pushed for new things to be built. Forests were hacked away, old homes brought low to kiss the ground they were built off of. Parking lots, superstores, and chain restaurants were being planned and built, a tombstone to what came before. The dead, however, refused to accept defeat.

Old artifacts cropped out from these sites, omens that Percival pushed aside for further progress. Since its inception, Helford was always a strange place. It was a hotbed for secret societies and filled to the brim with the esoteric. What was originally superstition for Helfordians, transformed into an outright aversion to the supernatural. To them, the best way to cope with the occult was to lock it away and bury the key. It worked for a while, but absence bred ignorance.

Many people warned Percival not to dig deeper, but he disregarded all of them. My uncle was the loudest.

"Don't forget, some things I hid on purpose," my uncle had always said to me.

It wasn't hard to imagine him saying the same to Percival.

One day, someone stranger than lies arrived in town. Gray sunken skin made tight by staples. Dark, old money suit tailored for a funeral. Red marks under eyes like fingernail scratches. Sparks flew off him and rippled over whatever he touched. It didn't take a genius to know he was beyond even the supernatural. He gave one reason and one reason only for being there: to speak with the mayor about the big changes being made.

Percival obliged with a self-satisfied grin. He had convinced a lot of people into things they would never accept otherwise. It'd be absurd to think that this stranger would be any different.

The story goes that Pervical invited the stranger into his home. Ten minutes passed, and the house exploded. Ground leapt into the sky. Glass and splinters rained onto the sidewalk. No one could have survived.

Yet, Percival did. He emerged from the resulting crater, and on the spot, gave up his job as mayor. The stranger was nowhere to be found. Helfordians got the message, taking the omen as another lesson why the supernatural should be hidden away at all costs.

All of this info was a shock for me. Local politics were a bloodbath. Though as Tomas told the story, one question crept through my mind.

"Whatever happened to Percival?"

"I don't know." Tomas shrugged.

"Really? You guys acted all mysterious over this incident, and you can't even tell me what happened to him?" I said.

"Look man, people didn't want to talk about him after all the occult stuff," Tomas said.

"Whatever. Let's get the creepy doll, I'm done waiting," I said.

Getting out of the car, Tomas and I walked our way to the back. Like a magician, I presented the trunk with as much fanfare as possible. Opening it, I revealed a bomber jacket, utility belt, a wooden case, and a creepy doll.

Tomas shielded his face from the doll. "Jeez, what is that?"

Porcelain skin and eyes that rattled in a still head. Its hands were set in place in a sort of fabric rigor mortis. I picked up the limp doll from the trunk. Despite how creepy it was, it had none of the qualities of a haunted doll described in my uncle's journal. Trust me, I checked.

"What?" I asked.

Tomas stepped away. "She looks like the victim of a divorce between two scary clowns."

"I named her Matilda," I said, brushing away fake hair. "Boo."

Tomas jumped. "Dude, quit it."

"Okay, I'll stop." I pulled my hands back. "But could you hold her while I get my dope new magic jacket on?"

Tomas glared at me. He sighed, grabbing the doll and holding it like a used diaper.

I presented the jacket to Tomas, showing each little detail of it.

"Quilted shoulders, six pockets, well insulated—"

"Yeah, yeah, but what's the magic part?" Tomas interrupted.

"Oh, right." I pointed at the strange sewing on the quilted parts of the jacket. "These symbols help to absorb any hits made against the jacket."

"Sweet, what's its limits?"

"That's for me to find out," I answered, putting on the jacket. "Now for the big reveal."

Lifting up the lid of the case, I displayed the same revolver I had shot myself with placed within a foam cast.

Carved into the barrel were the words "Final Line." Along with that read "Carnacki and Co." on the revolver's grip. Reading my uncle's journals, I discovered that this revolver has the unique ability to harm only monsters.

"You got ID for that?"

"Yes? It's a magic revolver so I don't know if you can even register it," I said.

Tomas went quiet, handing me the doll after I holstered the revolver.

"I'm gonna be arrested hanging out with you," Tomas said.

"Don't worry, the gun can't kill normal people. I checked."

Tomas gave me a side eye that would make anyone worried.

Running into the playground, we looked for a good place to put the doll. After a bit of confused running, we made our way to a spinning chair by the jungle gym. As I placed the doll, Tomas tugged at the back of my jacket.

"What?" I asked.

Tomas pointed over to the other side of the playground. A group of young kids were sitting by the slides, playing with their phones.

"Oh no, they're going to ruin the whole plan by being here," I said.

"Let's scare them away," Tomas said.

"Is that really the best way to go about this?" I asked.

"I dunno," Tomas shrugged.

I couldn't argue with that.

We walked over to the kids. All of them were around middle school age, the meanest age range. They were all drawn to their blue screens, playing some clicker game. Tomas cleared his throat, crossing his arms when the kids noticed.

"Sup," Tomas said with a deepened voice.

The closest kid looked side to side and over her shoulder. She had colorful bracelets running up and down her right arm.

Realizing we were talking to her, she responded, "Can I help you?"

"What are you three doing out so late?" Tomas said, pointing at the kids one at a time.

"Why does it matter to you?" the bracelet kid asked back.

"Nothing at all, just things are pretty dangerous around this time," Tomas said, hands in pockets.

I leaned into Tomas's ear and whispered, "What are you doing, man? You can't threaten children."

"I was?" Tomas whispered.

"Wait a minute," the farthest kid said. "I've seen you before."

Tomas and I went still.

"Oh yeah?" I said.

"Yeah, you're that weirdo two houses over from my house," the farthest kid said.

Tomas brought back the deep voice "What are you talking about? I'm no weirdo."

"Oh my god, he is," bracelet kid said.

The middle kid pulled a video from their phone, showing it to the rest of the kids. Peeking over a fence, it showed Tomas dancing in his old wizard garb, waving a stick in the air.

"Hey, that can be cool," Tomas said.

"It doesn't need to be cool, you just need to be," bracelet kid said back, the other kids erupting in laughter.

I stepped in, patting Tomas on the shoulder.

"Look, we're just trying to do something important, and we can't have you running around while it happens," I said.

"Is that your doll?" the middle kid said, pulling their phone out to record it.

"Yeah? Look, what can we do to get you to leave?" I asked them.

"So weird," the middle kid said.

Bracelet kid looked up, thinking. "Hm. A hundred bucks will do."

"Come on, what do you need a hundred bucks for?" I said.

"I don't know, but the cops would be asking you the same thing on why you're giving little kids money," the farthest kid said, the middle kid bringing their camera on me.

I sighed. "Okay, just delete the video and you have a deal."

"Deal," the kids said in unison.

I didn't have a hundred dollars with me, so Tomas and I spent a minute trying to pool some cash. As we pooled our cash, a strange shiver carried up my spine. I stopped, looking over to Tomas. He stopped, the same look painting his face.

"Dude," Tomas said.

"Yeah?" I said.

"In front of us."

A soft glow went over the three middle schoolers. Their eyes were looking through us. Their shoulders were sunken, their arms limp. They all had dropped their phones, the blue light put out by this new overbearing light.

Tomas and I hesitated to see what was over our shoulders, our heads struggling to turn past the strickening fear. The glow came from two hollow yellow eyes. Its light silhouetted a matted mess of seaweed-like hair. A basket rested at the creature's hip. It held three small children, who were gnawing at the air like piranhas.

More children orbited around her. Their eyes were milk white, sporting mouths filled with rows of teeth. They stood still waiting for their master's command.

"So, uh, you must be Basket Case." I said, "You're a lot taller than I hoped you'd be."

She remained silent.

"Okay, I guess we'll get going," I said.

The three middle schoolers leapt onto our backs. Wrapping around our necks, they attempted to hold us down. Two of the middle schoolers tackled Tomas to the ground. I held myself up, gripping onto the kid's wrists so she wouldn't strangle me.

With Basket Case's other children encroaching, I threw the kid off my back and over my shoulder. The middle schooler hit the wood chip floor, the other children stepping away to avoid her. The breath knocked out of her, she rolled about on the ground. My body froze. My mind was still processing what I had just done.

"Oh my god, did I?" I said.

"Screw them kids!" Tomas yelled.

Knocked from my thoughts, I ran over to pull the two other middle schoolers from Tomas. Once I freed him, I pushed the two kids into the crowd of evil children in front of us. Tomas shot up from his prone position, breathing heavily. He pulled out the shaver and looked at me.

"Do you trust me?" Tomas asked me.

"Does it matter?" I responded.

"Keep her occupied," he said.

Tomas and I split to flank the mass of monster kids. Basket Case's eyes followed my every move, ignoring Tomas. She might not know who I was, but she knew my uncle's jacket. The same jacket worn by a man who was a constant thorn in her side.

Basket Case stepped away, letting her ravenous children do the work of catching me. I got as close as I could, keeping their eyes focussed on me. Just as I got a few feet from Basket Case, a wave of kids tackled me to the floor. I blocked my face, as sharp teeth attempted to dig into my sleeves. The magic did its work, the kids unable to break any skin that my jacket protected. The parts it didn't protect, however, made me wish my uncle had instead bought a magically protected jumpsuit.

I tried to wrestle free, to no avail. Basket Case stepped closer and closer to me. Her glowing eyes enveloped my entire view. Breaking part of my guard, my right hand reached for the ground and grabbed a handful of wood chips. When my arm was free, I threw the wood chips into the eyes of Basket Case.

If life had taught me anything, it was to aim for the glowing thing. Basket Case lurched backwards as hundreds of tiny pieces lodged in her eyes. For the first time, I heard a sound come from her. A screeching sound like a mix between mice and scratching chalkboards from hell. She rubbed her eyes, her pain made manifest with each breath. Her children froze, getting up from the pile they made on top of me. They looked like they came awake from a half broken spell.

While Basket Case was distracted, Tomas activated his shaver. Shaving a big line of hair from Basket Case, Tomas grabbed whatever hair he could and ran towards the jungle gym. I ran with him.

Clearing her eyes, Basket Case took control of her children once again and sent them after us.

"Climb," I said to Tomas.

We climbed up to the top of the jungle gym. The children chased after us, their clawed hands attempting to bring us back to ground. Once at the top, I did my best to play defense. Any kid that got near Tomas, I would push or throw off. Soon the kids grew smart. They crawled inside the jungle gym, attempting to pull us down by our ankles to rip us limb from limb.

Stomping their fingers, I yelled to Tomas "Whatever you're doing, do it now!"

Tomas held a makeshift quartz amulet, Basket Case's hair tied in and around the string and crystal. Tomas closed his eyes and began to chant. At this point, Basket Case had left the killing to her children and was now transfixed on the creepy doll.

Each second Tomas chanted, the children gained more and more ground, filling the spaces of the jungle gym like fish in a net. Just as the children were welling up

71

towards us, Tomas finished his chant. A soft pink light blasted out from the gem. Recoiling from the crystal's light, the children scattered like a drop of water. Even Basket Case stepped away and blocked the light from her eyes. All her children cowered behind her, peeking their faces around her massive figure.

Having distance between us and her, I got ready to grab my pistol and fire at her. I wavered seeing the children surrounding her.

"What are you doing? Shoot her," Tomas said.

"I can't. What if I hit a kid? Are they technically monsters while under her spell? And if so, will my gun hurt them?"

Taking advantage of my hesitation, Basket Case began to devise her own spell. Her rasping voice echoed through the playground. Symbols, the same color as her eyes, flashed in the air like lightning bugs.

"Hey, can your spell counter whatever that is?" I asked Tomas.

"No, I'm not magic, Jonathan," Tomas said back.

"That's literally why I brought you here, Tomas," I said.

"I'm fighting her with bargain bin spells. I'm not that kind of magic!" Tomas said.

In between all of this, I realized I might die at a god-forsaken playground. A part of me wanted to give up and let whatever happens happen. Yet, I knew doing just about anything would be better than nothing.

I hopped off the top and yelled "Hey, Ms. Amber Alert."

Basket Case stopped her chant and put her attention back on me.

"I have no idea what I'm doing," I shouted.

"She is going to kill us," Tomas said.

"You don't think I know that?" I said to Tomas.

Putting my attention back on Basket Case, I continued. "You've known my uncle for a long time. He's brought the rain on your parade for the past decade. And seeing it now, I think I'll just end this whole cycle these idiots have put up with for their own gain. I may know nothing about you, but I do know beginner's luck. That's what I'm counting on. So come get me, you eight-foot soccer mom. I got one life to live."

Basket Case stared at me, and then at the porcelain doll I left her. She grabbed the doll and turned her back on me. The mad kid mob followed their mother, walking off into the darkness.

The air felt still, a cold chill hitting my forehead in waves.

"What the hell did you just do?" Tomas said.

I smiled, breathing in, then out. "Easy, I made her pity me."

# CHAPTER 6

Rule one about the pity maneuver, you can't use it on the same person twice. Next time we saw Basket Case, we'd have to play to win.

The next morning, Tomas and I went to work finding some way to melt our resident wicked witch of the west. Our first issue would be the children. We needed them out, and safe from Basket Case's control. My uncle had struggled for years finding a cure that would neutralize the spell Basket Case had over the children. He wasn't successful, instead choosing to keep the children under strict surveillance until the spell dissipated from them. Similar to detoxing, the process was difficult and time consuming.

He did however come up with a possible theory on how to cure Basket Case's little demon spawn. While sneaking through one of her old lairs, he found a special case. One made to hold a glass eye.

Having blinded Basket Case before, it made sense that her powers were in some way related to her sight. The glass eye could be the source of her power, since blinding her didn't fully break the spell. Maybe the spell was maintained because the glass eye still worked whether it had dirt on it or not.

Tomas said that with some prep time, he could have something ready to neutralize the eye. Main problem would be finding somewhere to put the prepared spell. The bigger the magic effect, the more complicated and less mobile the spell can be. It'd need to be real big to get to whatever kind of arcane mess Basket Case could cook up.

We ended up choosing to put it in the living room. We drew a massive chalk circle filled with interlocking patterns and sigils. Candles were placed at random around the border of the circle. Nothing could disturb the thing, so we needed to squeeze around it like Harriet's desk to get from one side of the living room to the other.

Mapping the current victims of Basket Case, we built a zone of activity for our big nanny from hell. We marked the center of the zone as a possible entry into Basket Case's lair and got ready to look for it around town.

We rented a van and filled the back with rope and other equipment to make exploring her lair easier. Once again, Tomas and I were doing a stakeout at night for the great and terrible Basket Case. The clock hit two and we were starting to feel the boredom bug set in.

"So, any plans for what to do with the money?" Tomas asked me.

"Well, we don't need to do anything with it other than buy groceries," I said, keeping my eyes on the binoculars.

"Oh, don't be like that, man. It's twelve thousand dollars, that's three whole zeros. We can have fun with it," Tomas said.

"What do you want with it?" I asked.

"Hm. Well, since we cleaned house, I was thinking we could redecorate."

I considered it for a second. "If we live through this, I'll let you redecorate."

"Yes." Tomas pumped his fists in victory.

As we kept watch, a man wandered around the crosswalk in front of us. Circling the area as if looking for something, his eyes eventually landed on the van. He walked straight towards us, tapping the passenger window. I rolled the window a hair's length down.

"Hey," the man said.

"Hey?" Tomas and I said.

"You, uh, you cops or something?" the man said.

Tomas looked at me confused. I shrugged.

78

Tomas turned back to the man. "Not that we know of."

"Yeah we're sitting in a van with binoculars for another reason," I said.

"Ah, great. I was standing at the corner to buy sneakers, and I don't want cops to think I'm..." the man gestured at the air. "You know."

He then laughed.

"Yeah, totally," I said.

"Nothing weird about that at all," Tomas said.

"Cool, great, yeah." The man paused for an uncomfortable amount of time. "You guys got tissues?"

"Yeah, sure," I said, trying my best to get rid of him.

Pulling a package of tissues out, I looked up to see the guy was gone. He had sprinted down the block and turned on one of the corners out of view.

"What the—" before I finished the sentence, Tomas pulled me down into the car's leg space.

I was about to curse Tomas out when a familiar yellow light hit the van's dash. Yellow eyes reflected off the mirrors, creeping closer with each wet thud. Like trumpets commemorating her arrival, the low growls of children soon followed. Their legs scurried on concrete. A few landed on top of the van, the sound rumbling the inside, us included. They crawled down the front window, sniffing at the air.

Basket Case's eyes went over the now empty front seats like spotlights. I held my breath, my body locking in place. Then the light left the car, the snarls becoming distant before disappearing.

Air entered my lungs again, my chest heavier than it was a few seconds ago. We pulled ourselves up, our plan coming back into focus. Slumped into my chair, I asked Tomas if he was ready.

"As I'll ever be," Tomas said, rolling up his sleeves.

Rolling out the doors, we ran to the back and grabbed all the equipment we'd need to face Basket Case. I lugged a backpack. A rope and a pair of heavy duty flashlights rustled inside. Tomas brandished his anti-Basket-Case amulet, humming his incantation as he ran.

We kept just out of ear shot, stalking her around whatever thing we could hide behind. The deeper into town, the more erratic her movements became. She followed the streets one way and bulldozed through fences on another. We were beginning to think she had lost it.

Stopping at a brick wall, she ran her hands across the rough surface. Her children played guard dog, watching her back for any intruders. They weren't very good spotters. We'd been hiding behind a row of mailboxes.

After moving her hand from one brick to another, Basket Case stepped away from the wall. A crack appeared down the middle of its mortar. The wall parted and slid open like a curtain. Beams of light crept from the opening, making it impossible to see what was inside. Basket Case disappeared into the light along with her children, the wall closing behind her. It clicked together like a puzzle piece, the crack resealing itself back to normal.

"Well, crap, I was hoping she lived in a hole or something," I said to Tomas.

We waited a few minutes, making sure she wouldn't catch us trying to open her door. Getting closer, we found no discernable symbols.

"Maybe it's activated by touch, like a trapdoor," I suggested.

I started running my hands over the brick, Tomas following suit.

"Wait a second," Tomas said.

I stopped.

Tomas pointed at one of the bricks. "Feel that."

I touched the brick. It felt colder than the others but was otherwise normal.

"It's a bit cold?" I said.

"Of course!" Tomas cheered.

"I'm not following."

"Oh sorry." Tomas collected himself. "This might sound a bit weird, but have you ever felt off before? Like when you're somewhere abandoned or holding something someone feels attached to?"

"Sometimes, why?" I said.

"Half of the time anyone ever gets that feeling, it's because of magic. Technically everyone can feel magic. It's kind of like instinct, but most can't identify why they feel it. That brick has a slight magic aura, so small that anyone unfamiliar with it wouldn't recognize it," Tomas explained.

Nodding along, I said, "You think adding magic to these areas could activate it."

"You're getting it now," Tomas said.

"Then let's get to it," I grinned.

I stepped back and let Tomas do his thing. With a better idea on what to look for, Tomas found each point of aura. Each one he found, he would add a small bit of his own magic to it. On the final point, the door activated. We shielded our eyes from the light as it opened.

Walking through, the light disappeared and we could see again. Inside was a massive complex, resembling a twisted dungeon. Torches lit the area. Brick archways lined the walls. We were closer to the ceiling than to the floor below. Beside us were stairs that led deeper into the underground complex.

There was no turning back at that point. Whatever we met down there, we would have to face it alone. I turned to Tomas, nodding if he was ready. He gave back a determined smile, nodding back. At least I had Tomas.

I took out the flashlights and we began the descent.

The stairs spiraled downwards. Pipes jutted out the corners, rusting and rotted. Beads of water sweated off the walls. The closer to the bottom, the darker it got. Soon the only sources of light were the ones we brought with us.

We wandered about, looking for where Basket Case could have gone. Tomas poked my back to get my attention. He pressed his finger against his lip, guiding me to one side of the wall. He waved one arm towards a dark area of the wall. In response, two torches lit parallel to each other. Hidden amongst the darkness was a hallway.

I stepped past Tomas, going deeper into the hall. After a certain increment, another set of torches would light the way. The further we went, the more it became apparent that the torches were revealing one thing and obscuring another. The ceiling and walls were pitch black. The only thing we could see was the path. I wasn't an expert in magic, but it wasn't crazy to imagine these torches working in bizarre ways.

"You think magic can make something like this?" I whispered to Tomas.

"Hard to say, none of this is really my ballpark," Tomas whispered back.

"Then we better learn quick."

We kept going, soon running out of torches to guide us.

"Dude, I can't see anything," Tomas said.

"Can't see…" I repeated back to myself.

I got a shot of inspiration.

"On the count of three, we both switch our lights off," I whispered to Tomas.

He nodded back.

"Alright, three."

Flicking the switch, we allowed ourselves to be drowned out by the darkness. The world turned quiet around us. I breathed in and out, closing my eyes. When I opened them, a pinprick of light appeared in my distant vision.

"Come on, that's our way out," I waved to Tomas.

"Huh, how'd you come up with that?" Tomas asked.

"She's a night creature, right? It's not crazy to think she designed her dungeon to cater to eyes that were used to darkness," I said.

Tomas patted my shoulder "And you said you were just short of clueless."

Good thing it was dark so Tomas couldn't see how red my face was.

The light grew as we got closer. The sound of rushing water filled our ears, a sign that we were going in the right direction. Making our way out the tunnel, the world was again illuminated.

This new room was massive, dwarfing anything I had been in before. Sewage pipes stuck out from the walls, water rushing out of them. Large moats carved into the ground collected this water around grates, forming whirlpools. Makeshift bridges were built, which I assumed were made to make crossing these moats less dangerous. Made from scavenged wood and PVC pipe, they looked ready to break at the slightest suggestion.

Taking this all in, the room still seemed to narrowly avoid feeling real. It could be heard and felt, yet still remained in the realm of dreams. Maybe it was the sewage gas talking, but something was telling me that none of this would exist without Basket Case.

We made our way over the first and second bridges, plastic pipes rattling under us. We were standing between two moats, when we heard a voice behind us.

"You made it a lot farther than expected."

Tomas and I swung around to meet the voice. A man, slightly older than us, stood at the first bridge we crossed. He wore a full black suit, and a smile too smug for its own good. His hair was platinum blond and curled into strange shapes above his head. Tomas was shocked to see him, and that was the only clue I needed.

"Percival Maelie, I assume," I said.

He smiled. "You're a damn fine guesser."

The hollow sound of feet on PVC came behind us, along with the scattering sounds of Basket Case's children army. We were trapped.

"It's great to meet Mr. Whitlock's second choice as successor."

"Second?" I repeated back.

Basket Case loomed over us as Percival spoke further.

"Indeed, but let's talk about this over tea. Who knows, it might save your life."

# CHAPTER 7

Judging from my limited experience, I'd say Basket Case had it good when it came to monster lairs. Stolen scaffolding surrounded the walls, which gave easy access to the exposed pipes built out of reach. This complex of pipes was used as convenient storage to hold both children and knick-knacks.

The focal point of the room was the circular table, which Basket Case used for tea parties. Porcelain children surrounded the table, each getting their own plastic chair. She even had Matilda, the doll I'd left her. They were the cleanest things in the room, and also the creepiest. Tomas was not having a good time.

We sat at the table, our butts sore sitting on plastic kids chairs. Percival sat across on his very own chair, elbows resting on the table. All the while, Basket Case prepared us tea. Using an electric kettle, she poured hot water into mugs. Everyone had an animal-shaped mug, apart from Basket Case, who had a mug in the shape of a baby's head. Tomas got a beaver, Percival a fox, and I got a crow.

Blowing away the steam, I took a sip of the tea. For a sewer creature, Basket Case had good taste in tea.

Basket Case responded with a muted nod.

"How long have you two been working as occult investigators?" Percival asked us.

"A few weeks," I said.

"Yeah, more or less," Tomas added.

Percival took a sip of his own tea. "Impressive. From how Basket Case described it, you two narrowly avoided being murdered by her."

"Doesn't seem like much of a compliment," I said.

"Wait, you can talk to her?" Tomas asked.

"In your line of work, it very much is." Percival then said to Tomas, "And yes, unlike you, I can understand her."

I looked around, trying to see what he could have gained from being here.

Percival noticed and answered, "I know it's difficult to imagine how any of this benefits me, lacking the bigger picture of it all."

"Context is very much appreciated," Tomas said.

"Let's just say I've been doing some soul-searching," Percival said.

"I'm sure the vapors here really helped," I said.

"Rest assured, Mr. Whitlock, I've not been held up in these sewers this entire time." Basket Case handed Percival a small pouch, which he placed in his coat pocket. "I've been exploring, making deals, and gaining the knowledge I need to succeed."

"And what does that success mean for everyone else?" I asked.

"At this point in your journey, I don't think you'd believe me if I was honest," he said.

Hearing that, I just stared at Percival. He didn't make sense to me. He'd been friendly to us, even more than his sister. Yet, speaking to him felt like downing shots of snake venom. He had a rug-pull waiting for us, I just couldn't tell what.

"Seems you already got it all accounted for, so what are you talking to us for?" I said.

"I'm only one man, Mr. Whitlock, and the supernatural world counts its dues in bodies. With your expertise, I could overcome what would otherwise be of great danger to me and my plans," Percival said.

"So you want us as lackeys?" I bit back.

"Yeah!" Tomas added with a dramatic flair.

"You'd be more than just that, believe me. Besides, you two are forgetting the situation you are in. The only real way out is through working with me, and I'm offering you rewards even after that," Percival said.

I eyed Percival's coat. The main power he had over us was knowledge. He knew what was going on in the town and in the supernatural world. Yet, he was desperate to work with us. He had to have known we were still new to this, so that couldn't be the real reason. There was some power we had over him, we just didn't know what that power was. I needed more information.

I crossed my arms, leaning back. "Show me what that pouch can do and then I'll think about us working together."

Percival's mood changed. His lips curved to a frown, and his brow furrowed. He sighed, and said, "If that's what convinces you, then fine."

Taking out the pouch, Percival revealed its contents. Inside was a fine glittering dust. Tomas gave me an uneasy look.

"It's called life dust, and it does this," Percival said

He tossed handfuls of the dust on the porcelain dolls strewn about the table. The dust settled on the dolls, covering them in sparkling shine. One by one the dolls jerked to life. Getting from their chairs, the dolls began moving about the room. They danced, drew with chalk, and wandered up scaffolding. They remained silent, their faces lacking the muscles to move lips. Basket Case watched, more interested with the dolls than the deal happening in front of her.

"Huh," I said under my breath.

"Dear hellfire, this is what nightmares are made of," Tomas said louder.

Tomas tried his best to stay away from the dolls, sitting with his legs tucked to his chest. Watching this weird display, I felt a tug on my jacket. It was Matilda, holding her arms out for an embrace. I picked her up, letting her rest on my knee. Tomas leaned forward and frowned at me.

"This is only a taste of what life dust can do. Now the choice is yours, leave with me or stay with her." Percival gestured at Basket Case.

I tapped my finger on the table, searching for some way to buy more time for Tomas and me to get out. We'd been stripped of all our weapons and had no running start. I was ready to cave to any demands he had when Matilda gave me a soft and comforting hug. At that moment, I had a plan.

"No, I don't think we'll work with you," I said.

Percival kept a straight face, while Tomas looked shocked and confused.

"Explain," Percival said.

"Yeah dude, please explain," Tomas said.

"I've seen what your sister was capable of. She could barely imagine doing anything useful with the time she had. It was all optics. You're no different, and I won't work with you like my uncle did," I said.

Percival went silent, his eyes square on my own.

"When I first saw you. I was a bit shocked. Not because of your skill or your circumstances. In fact, it was the opposite. I was underwhelmed. To see one of the greatest men I've known, now have his legacy get hijacked by someone with little to no drive is… disappointing. It seems those who make the world have to be born with it. Take care, Jonathan."

Percival adjusted his coat, got up, and disappeared out the door. Tomas lost his cool, begging for the former mayor to be more sparing.

"Hey, wait. I- I'm sure he'll reconsider if you just…" Tomas tugged at my jacket. "Jonathan, you'll think about it right? Jonathan? Aw, come on man!"

Basket Case didn't waste a second to drag us up the scaffolding and reward us with our very own prison cell. Plastic pipes were our prison bars, and a sewer pipe was our cell. I sat against the rusting walls.

Meanwhile, Tomas paced back and forth, refusing to talk to me. He had good reason to. I couldn't fill him in on the plan while Basket Case was in earshot. To him, I just sacrificed our lives for nothing. Time dragged on, and Tomas began complaining aloud.

"Why? Just why? Like what's your damage? We could have just agreed to work with him. Yeah I get it, gotta stick to morals and all that, plus he's a huge prick, but I'd rather listen to him drone on for the next year then starve to death in a sewer surrounded by creepy dolls!"

I let Tomas go on, instead using my time to watch Basket Case. After a while, his voice blended into the rest of the background static. Morning came and Basket Case dozed off, removing her right eye just before falling into deep sleep.

"Heck, we could have ditched him the moment he wasn't looking," Tomas went on.

I finally responded to Tomas, "That would've been the wrong move."

"How is that worse than being imprisoned by a literal hag?" Tomas exclaimed.

"Because for whatever reason, Percival needs us. The more we're in his periphery, the more likely he'll get exactly what he wants," I said.

Tomas crossed his arms. "He sure won't get anything from us dead."

"Exactly. If he thinks he left us for dead, he won't bother factoring us into his plans, giving us the wiggle room we need," I explained.

"Well that requires us escaping—" Tomas stopped when someone tapped on the bars.

It was Matilda holding Basket Case's eye along with all our equipment.

"—first," Tomas finished.

I gave Tomas a smirk.

"No," Tomas let out.

"Yep," I said back.

"I refuse."

"It's either escaping with her or staying here," I said.

"I hate you so much right now," he said.

"I had a feeling you would."

We suited up in the prison pipe, making sure everything was accounted for.

I presented Tomas with the glass eye, and said, "You think you can control the kids with this eye."

"In theory, yeah," Tomas said.

"Well in theory, we also have to rescue the kids," I said back.

Tomas rolled his eyes, grabbing the glass eye from my hand. The eye was an opaque yellow like a street light. It was smooth, but not in the way glass is smooth. The feeling was more similar to that of a rock or pearl. Tomas took out the quartz from his anti-Basket-Case talisman and replaced it with the eye.

Once the new talisman was ready, Tomas said, "We'll need to get to the ground floor, just to be sure she isn't awake to counter it."

I nodded, and Matilda unlocked the gate for us to leave. We tiptoed down the scaffolding, feeling out each step for possible groans or creaks. Our ears stayed alert for any disturbance in Basket Case's rest. We snuck over to the entrance.

Readying himself, Tomas whispered his incantation. The eye glowed softly, a slow hum emanating from it. My hand hovered over my pistol. My eyes switched between the amulet and Basket Case. As the chant droned on, sounds of movement came from the pipes above us. Swarming down like insects, children crawled out the pipes and down towards us. They stopped in front of us, sniffing at the air. Their bodies were still mutated and beast-like, eyes milky white.

Our mouths were wide open. It actually worked. We were about to jump in celebration when we noticed Basket Case turning in her sleep.

Slinking out of Basket Case's abode and into the wider sewage complex, we hoped to make it back to the hallway and up the stairway out. We went over the third and second bridge, the hallway close in sight. Yet, in that adrenaline state, through the sounds of rushing water, I could hear the sound of quiet chanting behind us.

"Get down!" I shouted.

Tomas and I ducked, a yellow fire bolt buzzing over us. Matilda and I dived one way while Tomas and the children dived the other. The bolt exploded where we were seconds before. I held tight to Matilda, using my body to cushion her fall. My vision became blurred, not helped by the fact my left ear was ringing.

The smoke cleared to reveal Basket Case. Her dolls stood guard around her. She gave off a low growl, her last eye glowing bright. The children swung and ran to Basket Case like moths to a flame.

Tomas stood back up and yelled "Oh no you don't."

Brandishing his amulet, Tomas made his own response to Basket Case's magic. The glass eye hummed louder, its light blinding. The children halted and raced back to Tomas. Basket Case wailed out with her arm outstretched. Her remaining eye matched the brightness of her stolen one, and the children again stood frozen. The children wandered back and forth, their minds in a magic tug of war.

Tomas strained, trying to pull the children to his side, his legs close to giving out from under him. With each passing second, the children came closer under the hag's control.

As Tomas struggled, I knew I had one final line of defense. I pulled out my uncle's pistol and aimed it at Basket Case. My hands shook, the tremors making aim almost impossible. My breathing became uneasy, and doubt shattered my concentration.

Doom was ready to set in, when Matilda leaned into my periphery. The little porcelain doll patted her small hand against my shoulder, her best attempt at comforting me. She directed me with her other hand, pointing it at Basket Case's head. I aimed my gun where she was pointing, pulled back the hammer and then finally the trigger. The gun kicked back, its bullet cracking the air around it.

Whizzing past the two bridges, the bullet went into Basket Case's only eye. It popped, and a light squelching sound echoed out. Shutting her socket to hold in her destroyed eye, Basket Case curled and shrieked. Her hand pressed over her eye, her body collapsing onto the cold floor, shuddering.

I took in a deep breath, relief rushing into me. The children, now under Tomas's control, surged over to him. Right when we were starting to feel hopeful, the ground under us began shaking.

Cracks formed on the ground and ceiling, pieces of bricking falling out and unto us. Picking up Matilda, I ran with Tomas towards the hallway entrance. Tomas went in first with all the children. Before I followed him, I turned to get one last look at Basket Case.

Her dolls surrounded her. Each of them attempted to comfort her as Matilda did to me. She stayed curled on the ground, quivering. As the roof collapsed down on them, the dolls stared back at me. I left soon after.

Running down the hallway, we made our way up the stairway that led out. I stayed behind with Matilda, making sure there were no stragglers. Stammering up the stairs, we stopped at the wall as Tomas tried to do the wall puzzle.

"Oh god, was it that brick? Or that one?"

"Anytime now, Tomas," I said.

"That one... then... there!" Tomas said, pressing the last brick.

The door opened at a crawling speed. With the ceiling ready to go down, we had all the children leave first. Tomas and I jumped through, the ceiling collapsing behind us. Hitting the ground, both of us groaned out in pain.

Rolling onto our backs, we presented our tired faces to the blue morning sky. Clouds rolled through, the sun cutting past it all. Our brains began to settle. I started laughing, and Tomas joined in. Rolling in dirt and gravel, we kept laughing, happy to be alive.

# CHAPTER 8

The wicked witch was dead, and there was still more for us to do. First up was making that army of monstrous kids a bit less literal.

We decided to leave the kids in the van while we did the ritual to change them back to normal. It was easier for us, since we would be taking them back as soon as the ritual ran its course. It did take us a while to finish it, or rather it took a while for Tomas to. Poor guy had to sit in one place for four hours, doing nothing except chanting.

All that time to kill gave me a moment to think. Something hadn't felt quite right. We had won, but I still felt like we weren't really the heroes for it. I pulled the mayor's still fresh check from my pocket. I took a good look at it. It was marked by someone who kisses babies while signing death warrants. I never liked having filth as bedfellows, and I wasn't going to start with her.

Finishing the ritual, we got to returning the kids back to their parents. It wasn't easy, most of the kids having damaged or lost phones. We drove all across town, delivering one child after another.

About halfway through delivering all the kids, we happened upon city hall on the way to meeting with another parent. I asked Tomas if we could make a stop there, saying I had to have a word with the good mayor. Which wasn't too far off.

Busting through her door, I slammed Maelie's check flat on her stone slab of a desk. She looked up at me confused.

"Deals off, Maelie," I said.

"Off how?" she stammered.

"I'm not gonna be a part of your political stunt," I said.

"What about Basket Case?" she asked.

"Dead as far as I know," I said.

"What!" Maelie stood up, changing her tune in a heartbeat. "I mean, what a relief. She was such a plague on this town."

"Glad you agree. Consider it charity," I said.

I headed for the door, when Maelie said, "You're really gonna leave after that? The election. My campaign. You know what this means for our business relationship?"

"This doesn't really mean anything. Think about it. Try to find someone who can do the things my uncle and I can do. I doubt you will," I responded.

Maelie went quiet.

"Yeah, you know my number," I said.

"This isn't over, Whitlock. I'll find someone! You hear me!" she shouted before I shut the door on her.

I was surprised that Tomas wasn't pissed when I told him I turned the money down. He just gripped the steering wheel hard, and then sighed. He was, however, disappointed to not have a chance to redecorate like he wanted.

When I asked him why, he said, "You know, I thought you lost your mind in those sewers. To me you were risking our lives over things we had no business in. But then I remembered my mom, and how she'd react if I up-and-disappeared one day. Made me a bit less mad, knowing we were helping people who had dealt with that."

I sat in the passenger's side, quiet.

"Just tell me what you're planning first, man," Tomas added.

"Yeah, let's make group huddles mandatory before each mission."

"Dude, that's what I'm saying," Tomas said.

Our last stop was an antique store, owned by the grandparents of one of the children. It was night, and everyone involved was exhausted. Tomas chose to stay in the car, while I brought the kid to the grandparents. As the kid reunited with her grandparents, one of them asked how they could ever repay me. I looked at Tomas, and then at shelves lined head to toe in antiques.

"Actually, I can think of something."

It goes without saying that Mr. Armageddon went crazy with decorating. Framed posters of old magicians lined the living room walls. Beside the couch was a display with a monkey's paw inside. In one corner was a life-like statue of a sasquatch, across from it a replica of a sarcophagus. As revenge for me getting Matilda, Tomas left a clown mannequin in my room. He got what he wanted. I couldn't even open my eyes without that thing scaring the hell out of me.

It seemed like this week's problems were settled, all except one.

"Do we really need to keep her?" Tomas said as he watched Matilda.

Sitting crisscrossed on the living room floor, Matilda drew on the white board we gave her to communicate with. Tomas sat on the couch, trying to be comfortable with Matilda there too.

"Are you sure about this? I'm sure a retirement home would love her," Tomas added.

"Yep, she helped us escape, so she's basically a part of the team now."

Tomas grimaced at me, and then at Matilda. We were about to fall back into silence, when a question came to mind.

"You know, we never found out what Percival was planning next," I said.

"How could we? He was being pretty vague about the whole thing," Tomas said.

"I don't know, all I'm asking for is one extra clue." As I said that, Matilda got up with her whiteboard and walked towards me.

Writing with purple Sharpie, Matilda said, "I know."

I sat up from my seat "You do?"

Matilda nodded.

"How?" I asked.

Matilda wrote down, "I remember before life."

"Before life? So you remember your existence before you were given life?" I asked.

Matilda nodded, writing, "He talks a lot."

I snickered, "He does, doesn't he?"

"Wait, if you remember hearing your surroundings before being alive, does that mean you remember what I—" Tomas went quiet.

Matilda showed her board to Tomas, and wrote, "It's okay, you didn't know."

"Still, I'm sorry," Tomas said.

Matilda went over and hugged Tomas. As expected, Tomas bunched up the moment she did. He didn't hug her back, and it wasn't hard to see he was waiting for her to stop.

"What did you overhear? Any words or details that come to mind."

Matilda drew on her board, "Revival Festival."

"Revival Festival? What would he be doing at that?" Tomas queried.

"You know what that is?" I asked Tomas.

"Yeah, it's pretty cool. You dress up how you want and go around and do stuff," Tomas said.

"When does it happen?" I said.

"Every November," said Tomas. "Oh, we should go. We can theme our clothes together."

"That's in two weeks… If that's where Percival is going, then yeah let's go to Revival Fest," I said.

"Yes! I'll get the sewing machine."

Now we had something to go off. Get into Revival Fest and collect clues to find out what Percival Maelie was up to. Also maybe have fun while we're at it.

# CHAPTER 9

First rule about Revival Fest: never, under any circumstances, talk about Revival Fest. If a Helfordian talks about Revival Fest, then they aren't actually Helfordian. Imagine that, the biggest holiday in Helford, and on most days of the year people act like it doesn't exist. It's a tough shell to crack, but damn if it ain't a sight to see in person.

We stood at the entrance of Revival Fest, a red gateway with a small toll booth right beside it. Massive wood palisades obscured the entire area, resembling an old colonial-era fort. It seemed a bit redundant since the place was already so out of the way. The holiday was held deep in the Dipperty-Mabel forests, Helford's oldest and biggest forest. Getting here was hell, with the only way there being over an underdeveloped road either by car or foot. Not to mention Revival Fest happens only during the dead of night.

In classic Revival Fest tradition, both Tomas and I dressed up. Tomas dressed as a warlock, complete with dark cloak and pointy hat. He had his old staff decorated to look like a broom. Tomas even managed to find glow in the dark make-up, making parts of his face glow a ghastly green.

To fit the theme we had, I dressed as a warlock hunter. I also wore a strange hat and cloak, though mine had more buckles to fit the pilgrim aesthetic. A bandolier went across my chest, holding four sheathed daggers. I held onto Matilda, who was dressed as a voodoo doll.

"Does my hat look better on this or that side?" Tomas said.

They looked the same. "I think that side's best."

Tomas again reshuffled his hat.

We approached the toll booth. Sitting inside was a man dressed as a jester. His hat, lined head to toe in bells, jangled with each little inflection he made.

"Tickets, please," he said.

I looked at Tomas, confused. No one told us we needed tickets. As we checked our pockets for a ticket, the Jester laughed.

"Ah, I'm just messing with you two, you can go on ahead," he said.

"Really?" I said.

"Why not? You're clearly Helfordians by the way you stand," he laughed.

"The way we stand?" I asked.

"Look, don't get into the details too much. Have fun and remember that what you bring inside will give you no power in there. All are equal in that way," he said.

"What do you mean by that?" I asked further.

The jester looked at me and then said to Tomas. "This man brings all the questions, doesn't he?"

"You have no idea," Tomas said.

Insulted, I said, "I'm just asking questions because this is doubling as an investigation."

"Investigation?" The Jester snorted. "Here? Good luck with that."

"Whatever. Let's go, Tomas," I said.

Just before we entered the Revival Fest, the Jester leaned out his booth and added, "Hey wait, didn't mean to put you in a bad mood. Here's something for your troubles. Find Trellis. He'll show you the ropes so you can get around better."

"Trellis? I don't know who that guy is, but thank you?" I said.

"Have a good Revival Fest my friend," the Jester said, grinning.

Piercing the entrance's dark veil, we were opened to the complex world of Revival Fest. It was a muddy trail, imprinted by a thousand souls. Worn masks gleamed under red lantern light. Smiles etched in spray paint and paper mache. It's where someone in a tunic and green hood could dance with people wearing bell bottoms and psychedelics. Flappers, hippies, knights, and Greek philosophers all passed by us as we walked.

"Maybe theming wasn't going to be our biggest issue," I remarked.

"Hey man, don't discount how dope we look," Tomas said.

"We do look really cool," I said, then added, "I am wondering how we'll find Trellis with all this going on. Maybe he's a manager or planner of some sort, or even a vendor."

"I guess we'll have to— ooh, what's that?" Tomas said, walking over to one of the vendors.

"Hey, don't get distracted," I said, running after Tomas.

We did in fact get distracted. Perusing everything we could, we hopscotched from vendor to vendor. The items ranged from strange niche products to high-priced souvenirs. One vendor in the same breath tried to sell us both sabers and scented soaps. Before we dived into shopping, we both promised to not spend our money on anything too dumb. That soon became a guideline rather than a set-in-stone rule.

One tent we came across, lined up and down with books, was run by a strange dark robed man. His voice was deeper than the Mariana Trench. Each echoing word carried its own zip code, his face indiscernible under a shrouded hood. Tomas left with a book, costing him a whopping ninety-nine bucks. As it turns out, the mysterious man was an excellent salesman.

"Basics in Thaumaturgic Theory," the title read.

"I thought you already knew the basics of magic," I said.

"Yeah, barely. I only had a few protection spells to use against Basket Case. Who knows what firepower we'll need for next time," Tomas said.

"You think that has what you'll need?" I asked.

"That's what the guy said," Tomas said.

"I guess if you're getting something, I should too," I said.

Scanning the area where we were, I saw one tent that peaked my interest. The front was covered by a quilted blanket, with a wood board reading "The Loot Box." A certain allure came with that name, along with a repressed gambling addiction.

We entered the tent, welcomed in by an old woman. Inside were crates filled to the brim with miscellaneous items. It looked like a hoarder's heaven.

"Ah, great, nice to see a fellow witch among all the sorry saps here," the lady said, moving away from a mountain of garbage.

Tomas and I glanced at each other. Then we both realized what she meant.

"Oh I'm not a witch," Tomas said. "I'm a warlock."

"Then what's with the hat?" she asked, waddling over to us.

Tomas pointed to his hat. "The hat isn't pointy enough to be a witch hat."

"Yeah sure, buddy," the lady said, giving a disregarding wave of her hand.

"If I'm not a warlock, then what is he?" Tomas pointed to me.

"Well obviously he's a warlock hunter," she said.

"Then how does that make me not a warlock?" Tomas exclaimed.

She gave another wave. "Eh, whatever you say. What do ya' want?"

"We saw the name, and we're wondering what that's all about," I said.

The lady smirked, rubbing her hands with devilish intent. "Ah yes, the Loot Box. How'd you feel about hearing a little story from yours truly?"

"Actually we're kind of in a—"

The old lady interrupted me. "It all started in the crazy seventies. The drugs were great and my sex life still had some more years to go. I was your typical muse, speaking as a prophet to the future, when I had the most novel idea. The loot box!"

The lady rustled through a box, pulling a pack of tarot cards. Blowing the dust off, she shuffled as she explained further.

"To be quick and simple about it, I read your immediate future and the problems that come with it. Then

I give you a box of whatever I got that can help solve those problems. Boom. Loot box."

"So you charge us for the items you give us?" I asked.

"Uh huh," she said.

"Do you tell us which items solve what problem?" I asked.

"Nope, you gotta find that out yourself," she said.

"Wait... couldn't you just sell the future predictions so people can just avoid the issue all together?" I asked.

"You know that would seem reasonable," she said, bowing her head. She then smacked me over the head with a ladle. "For a doofus who can't read the future."

"Of course they'd still have to deal with the problem. You ever seen someone plan for everything and still manage to mess up? Of course you have. That's called being alive. Best you can do is give people the proper tools to handle it how they can. You can't avoid it, otherwise we wouldn't call it fate."

I rubbed my aching head. "You didn't need to hit me to tell me that."

"Psh, I don't need cards to know that you, buster, are bullheaded." She began to organize her cards. "So you want to face your fate or not."

"Sure, I'll bite. How does it work?" I said.

The lady gave that grin people give before the punchline to a joke. "How many items are you looking at getting?" she asked.

"Three? I don't have a reference," I said.

"I'll get you four," She said, grinning.

As she shuffled, past muses egged her on, whispering little secrets into the cards.

"Ooh momma, come on, give me something good. Let's get interesting," she said.

Four cards made their grand entrance, shooting out and sliding across a table a few feet away. Waddling over, she picked up the four cards.

Studying the cards, she nodded with pursed lips. "Now this is interesting. A Tower and Devil card, along with reversed Temperance and Magician cards."

"What do they mean?" I said.

"Not yet, future vision is still cooking," she said, explaining. "The cards are a visual tool. To help see the river instead of the ocean… and there's your fate."

Slinking over to one side of the room, the lady grabbed what looked to be a mix between knife and boomerang.

"That's for the reversed Magician."

Jamming her hand in a box beside her, she pulled out a spiraling lollipop the size of my head. It was fresh, wrapped by clear plastic.

"The Devil," she said, darting her head around for the last two items "Aha!"

Crouching down, she came out lugging a boombox.

"Here's a cassette of 2002's best Christian hip hop hits. That's for the reverse Temperance," she said.

"Thanks?" I said.

"Welp, that'll be seventy bucks," she said, clasping her hands.

As she wandered off to the register, I stammered, "Wait, what about the Tower card?"

She smiled "You see, the fourth item was within you the whole time."

I looked at her, this small woman who looked eighty on a good day. Frazzled white hair on a sock puppet face. Eyes rattling with each assured nod. Only one thing was on my mind.

"I'm paying seventy for that?" I said.

"Aw please, it's a good deal. Besides, you already paid," she said,

"I did?" I said.

"Yeah, I grabbed your card while you were looking into space like a total dork," she said, laughing.

"No way, you can't without my—"

"Future powers," she blurted.

"This is absurd, this is worse than when I got fleeced by middle schoolers," I said.

"Now that's just sad, get going before I start catching your mopiness," the lady said.

Herded out the store, Tomas and I stood in total shock. We shuffled in place, unsure what to do.

"Now what?" Tomas asked me.

I couldn't give a good answer. Instead I eyed the puddle just in front of us. My reflection stared back, just as clueless as I was, until it was erased away by the rippling reverberations of distant music. I looked up, trying to see where the music came from. A circus tent was nestled in a distant corner. Its insides lit up with strobe lights. The crimson stripe outside swayed back and forth with the beat.

"Guess it's time to quit and join the circus," I said under my breath.

Up close, the circus tent was a modern-day colosseum. A line of people flowed in, while another line stumbled out. Tomas and I stood in line, sandwiched between a group of dapper skeletons and Victorian maids. We did have a situation where a raving disco man grabbed onto me, hollering about reptilians ruling everything. He got dragged away by a group of robed men a few seconds after.

Inside the tent, hedonism sat at its throne, laughing. People danced, drank, and did pills the colors of rainbows. Platforms led to venues where things went even further. Partygoers rolled off platforms and down stairs in ways that folded the mind into shapes like origami. All of this happening in an ocean of noise and movement. Each step forward required planning weeks in advance just to avoid stepping on someone.

Going to the lowest platform, we found ourselves at a bar where a man dressed as Dracula served drinks. Tomas gestured me to get closer.

"I can get some drinks," he yelled in my ear.

I nodded in agreement. As he went to the bar, I sat a bit at the far edge of the platform. I took a second to breathe, closing my eyes. It lasted for about a second before I was pushed awake by someone dressed in the old masquerade style.

"Can I help you?" I asked.

"Psst, it's me," the person said, taking off the mask to reveal Mayor Harriet Maelie.

Her cheeks were a bright red, which was noticeable even under the tent's deep tints. She gave a sly smile, which further told me that she wasn't all there.

She placed the mask back on, mumbling, "How ya doin? Been a long time since you ruined my chances in the next election."

"Ruined your chances? How does one canceled photoshoot with kids ruin an election?" I said.

"Well when your family's campaign slogan has been 'Keeping the same days rolling' for the last decade, you start to get desperate for some decent PR… but I forgive you. So how's it hanging, buddyroo?"

She squeezed between me and someone else. Of all the people I wanted to see here, Harriet was not on that list. Basket Case was higher up on that list than she was. I felt dirty just sitting by her. I gave a crooked smile, nodding that I was good.

"I knew you would be." she said, her mind drifting off as she spoke.

Regaining consciousness, she hopped to a whole other train of thought. "It's great you know… Here and all. Actually not really. I'm not doing fine."

I looked over to Tomas, who was still looking at the drink menu. I wanted to get up and leave, but the dance floor would have been harder to navigate than her conversations.

"What's wrong?" I said.

Harriet leaned against the booth. Her mask pointed up to the massive disco ball hanging in the center.

"I feel like I'm becoming my father," she said,

I took a second to process that. "I'm sorry… what?"

"Sounds stupid, right? Big Mayor Maelie is getting scared like the rest of the sheep, but I am. You wanna know a secret? I didn't even want to be mayor," she said.

"Really?"

"Yep, and whatever is said in Revival Fest, stays in Revival Fest. Good luck telling anybody," she said.

"I wasn't planning to," I said.

"Good, you know how to keep your mouth shut. Just like me and the rest of my family." Maelie went quiet, head slumped. She revved back to life the moment I was feeling comfortable again. "I didn't even want to be mayor. I wanted to be a school counselor. Help people. That sort of thing."

That part shocked me, seeing how she felt about me saving those kids from an eternity in the sewers.

"But that's not how the Maelies run. We're a machine. An engine that runs no matter what. If a gear gets out of line, they drop it and replace it without a second thought," she said.

I nodded as she spoke, responding, "Guess that's what happened to your brother."

"We're not allowed to talk about him. Not because he did something we wouldn't do, but because he wanted to take it further. We're an engine, but god help us if we use it for anything."

Thinking some more, I asked, "Did your brother tell you anything before leaving?"

Maelie paused, then said, "Not anything you should know."

That made me curious.

"Sounds like something your father would say," I said.

I sat still and let those words settle amongst the whooping bass and strobe lights.

She took the bait like I hoped, saying, "I don't know… said something about seeing some big bad secret society. Made a whole thing about it being the key to something."

"What key?" I asked.

Harriet let out an annoyed groan. "Too many questions. I'm here to have fun."

"Can I ask just one more?" I said.

"If it's the last, then yeah," she said.

"You seen anyone by the name of Trellis around here?" I asked.

"Oh yeah, he's at the highest platform. Big goat horns, can't miss him." Harriet tried to hold in a burp. "He's great."

I turned and craned my head to see the stark ascent to the tallest platform.

"Dude, you have no idea how long it took to get these. I didn't know what you wanted, so I just got you what I got," Tomas said behind me.

I rolled back around, and saw that Tomas was holding two colorful plastic martini glasses. I thanked Tomas and we clinked glasses.

"Up to anything while I was gone?" Tomas asked.

"Oh yeah, I was just talking to—" I turned to see that Harriet was gone.

I looked around, only to hear the sound of someone yelping and falling down a flight of stairs. Wherever she was going now, she was going to feel it all of next week.

"I guess not," I said. "Let's get going. I think we found our lead."

# CHAPTER 10

Trellis, the fool, the myth, the legend. His horns extended from his forehead and curved to form a Fibonacci spiral, the kind found all over nature. He lay reclined on a sea of pillows, arms around a woman and a man. His eyes were half opened from what seemed to be a mix of both self-assuredness and psychoactive drugs.

The crowd around him was a different breed than the others we passed by on our way up. They knew something. Secrets hidden with a layer of skin and painted over with the soft hues of LED lights. They stood like statues, moving only their heads as we approached.

"Cool to see another Whitlock grace my presence so soon after the last one fell in his ivory tower," Trellis said.

Clocking my shocked expression, he added, "It's all in the eyes. He had them as well. Too determined to live comfortably. I never understood those kinds of eyes. It's like you only live by fighting words. I guess I can't blame you, can I? Seems to be genetic."

"You knew my uncle?" I asked.

"Wow, my first guess was that you were his long lost son or something. Makes sense, he wasn't really about kids or relationships. He was always running around with his little apprentice whose name I can't for the life of me remember. So what do you need? Or are you just here to party? 'Cause if so, you're already much more fun than your uncle."

"I'd love to, but I'm trying to find something out. Someone said you'd be able to help me with that," I said.

Trellis looked at me, disappointed, sighed and said, "I guess that's genetic too. What is it then?"

"One of the Maelies, Percival Maelie, is after something in Revival Fest. Something about a secret society. I'm hoping you know what it might be."

Scrunching his face, Trellis asked us, "Have you ever met the main coordinators of Revival Fest?"

We both shook our heads. Matilda wrote "No" in bold text.

"Well that's because there aren't any. At the very least not any that are human," Trellis said.

"Then how was this all set up?" I asked.

Pulling himself onto his feet, he said, "Walk with me and I'll show you."

He took us outside. Parting the river of people, he walked to a wall with a good view of the pathway.

We got a better view of Trellis. He was heavy set, his wife beater not helping to hide that fact. He sported pink sandals, which matched well with his jean shorts. Two colorful hearts were sewn into the back of his shorts, one for each buttcheek. Unendingly charming, everyone that passed us either laughed or blushed seeing him.

I felt a sneaking suspicion there was more to that.

"Dealing with Basket Case, I've seen the effects glamor can do to someone," I said.

"That's all me, baby. I don't need magic to be the light of the party. You're just too square to feel that. If you wanna see real magic, I'll gladly give you a taste," he said.

That last part sounded like a threat. Basket Case had shown me how dangerous the supernatural could be, and I wasn't about to be caught off guard again. I was on edge, ready to fight if needed. That was until he said, "You ever heard of the origins of Revival Fest?"

Tomas and I both said "No."

"A long time ago, when Helford wasn't the city all of you know, a new revivalist movement was being made nationwide. You see, a bunch of chuds started getting the idea that the US wasn't close enough to god. People were having too much fun in their big city on a hill, so they made that everyone else's problem. That idea hit Helford hard. Everyone started clutching their pearls and making a big fuss about satanic influences. That is to say, having a good time. The people who suffered the most from that were the immigrants who moved to Helford for a new chance at life. Still carrying their old folk ideas from overseas, these immigrants needed a way to practice their ideas without being persecuted."

"And that's where Revival Fest comes in?" I asked.

"Bingo, all the immigrants ended up taking their beliefs deep in the forest and practicing them in the dead of the night," Trellis said.

"But how did it become such a big deal, if it was made in secret for such a small group of people?" Tomas asked.

"That's where the interesting part happens. When the people who so reviled these folk beliefs found out about

Revival Fest, instead of destroying it or banning it, they went themselves, in secret. Everyone has a wild side, some of them are just more ashamed of it. After a while, the celebration became a thing for all of Helford, synthesizing the self-ashamed secrecy of Christian Revivalism with the Spiritual beliefs of peasants off the boat from Europe."

Trellis dug into his pockets, pulling out a blunt. Lighting it up with his fingers, he almost inhaled the entire blunt with his first drag.

Puffing out a massive cloud, he said, "Imagine an app, where you could search up something and find exactly what you needed."

Tomas tried to explain, but it just came out as "Well, um... uh. . ."

I intervened, saying, "Yeah they already invented that."

"It's a good idea though," Tomas added.

"Oh damn." Trellis looked into space. "What was I talking about?

"About who runs the park," I said.

"Oh yeah, no one does," he said, explaining. "There's no need to. To make it simple, when the immigrants came, they brought not just their superstitions but their own creatures. These creatures soon partook in the festivities, making their own stake into it. A beacon for all monsters. Over time, Revival Fest became its own beast."

"You're saying Revival Fest is alive?" I asked.

"Somewhat. It's complicated. It can change, manipulate and attract. It seems to even enjoy people, but to a point. It's as complex as any living being can be," Trellis said.

"That's cool and all, but it doesn't answer my question about Percival," I said.

"That's because I don't know." He took another hit from his blunt. "But I know who does."

"Who would that be?" I asked.

Trellis looked me up and down. Giving a wide smirk, he started to laugh. He kept on laughing. Any time he'd lay his eyes on me, he'd laugh. Over and over.

"You're gonna hate this so goddamn much," he wheezed.

He was right.

"God damn it!" I shouted as I stormed away from Trellis.

"Dude, it's not that bad," Tomas said, trying his best to keep up the pace.

"Isn't it? We already had no idea about what to do next. Now you're telling me we gotta go on some vague vision quest?" I said.

"Look, man, I didn't say it was easy," Tomas said. "You're acting like this is the end of the world. I should know, I tried that once. All we need to do is party hard enough to connect with Revival Fest and learn what we need to find Percival."

"You make that sound easy," I said.

"And you make having fun sound impossible," Tomas said.

Swinging to Tomas, I said, "Maybe it is to me. Ever thought of that, huh?"

Tomas glowered at me, unimpressed.

"Drama queen," Tomas said under his breath.

I opened my mouth, but stopped before I started saying anything I would regret. Tomas's glower stopped and changed instead to concern.

Trellis told us that the only one who could help us now was Revival Fest itself. The only way to communicate with Revival Fest was to be what the festival itself represented. We would have to be debaucherous, free thinking, and most importantly honest with ourselves.

"Remember what we talked about after Basket Case? We're a team and we need to talk about these things," Tomas said.

I took a second to think, and said, "Trellis was right. I've never been good at partying. I get in my head, and always end up having less fun than I should have. I can have fun walking around, but doing what they do? I just don't have that kind of energy."

Telling Tomas that made me feel like a kid again in all the worst ways. I got smaller, the ground sinking so I was closer to its level. The world centered itself on me like the crosshairs of a sniper rifle. One pull of that trigger and I was done for.

I was about to run to the hills, when Tomas placed his hand on shoulder. At that moment, time slowed to normal. My surroundings became clearer and less abstract. We were by the food court, the air smelling of funnel cakes and hotdogs.

"I can't understand everything going on in your head, but I can understand this. You learn fast, faster than anyone I've met in Helford. I mean, come on? You've wrapped your head around crazier things. What you need now is for someone to show you the ropes, and for that, I'm your man." Tomas pointed to himself, eyes filled with determination.

"You are?" I asked.

"Yeah, I've partied like you wouldn't believe. I even got a doctor's note telling people to stop inviting me to ragers."

"That doesn't sound real," I said.

"I think about that every time I wake up in the morning, but that's not the point." Wrapping his arm over my shoulder, Tomas guided me to the food court. "Your biggest issue right now is that you want too much control. You want to plan and build systems, when that's never how things like these are supposed to work."

"I know that, but what else am I supposed to do? How do I know when it's right to do something? When should I eat? When should I drink? When should I put the chairs away?" I asked.

"Chairs? That sounds crazy even to me. Think about this, when do you drink water?"

"When I'm thirsty," I said.

"Yuh huh. And did you plan when you were going to be thirsty?"

"Of course not, that's not how that works," I said.

"Yeah, same thing with Revival Fest and any other party you're at. You do what you feel, not what you think you should feel. That's how a party can start out loud, get violent, then get heartfelt, and end quietly all in one night. Once you get that, you'll become unstoppable. So answer me this, what do you want?"

My stomach growled. "I'm kind of craving some french fries, and maybe a corndog."

"Then let's get some," Tomas said.

We did that, eating fresh fries with a corndog lined with ketchup and mustard. It was amazing after all that walking around. I described the taste to Matilda, giving her some way to imagine what eating is like. She enjoyed the descriptions, saying they sounded delicious. When we were finished, Tomas asked me what I wanted to do next.

In the distance, a body-builder swung a log ride back and forth like a pendulum.

"I bet I'd last longer on that than you," I said.

"Dude, you're on," Tomas responded.

A minute later, I was laying on a pile of trash. Tomas stood over me. He held Matilda at arm's length like she was the trash I was currently in.

"Dang, he launched you like a satellite," Tomas said.

"He did look like he seasoned his protein with more protein," I said.

"He did!" Tomas sat crisscrossed beside me. "What do you want to do now?"

"A drink is sounding real good right now."

Buying some drinks, Tomas asked me what I wanted to do. I told him and he would ask me the same thing again and again all night long.

# CHAPTER 11

We hit the dance floor harder than the asteroid that killed the dinosaurs. Tomas was smooth about it, acting like he'd been there since the dawn of time. I ended up knee sliding so hard I invented a new sport. I called it human bowling. It was fun as the bowling ball, not so much as the pins.

One drink, two drinks, green drink, blue drink, we had it all. At first it went down like flavored hand sanitizer but got better the more we had. My legs got heavier, having the nimbleness of uneven ladders.

I answered every question with a "Yes," no matter how insane it was. One person asked me what time I would die. For some reason, I knew the answer.

We coasted from one party to another, making sure to do whatever event or game was on the way.

At the food court, Tomas took some time skimming his new book. Chapter by chapter he'd read, finding some new facts to be giddy about. I munched on a cone of tiger blood shaved ice, whatever that was, and nodded along.

It was nice watching him be so interested in something. To see his smile creep up before blessing me with new facts. To feel his knee thump the table from all the built up excitement. I couldn't help but feel happy about the book too.

"Dude, I've been doing it all wrong," Tomas said.

"You were? Seemed to me you were throwing around fire just fine," I said with a mouthful of slush.

"Well I was, but not in a way I should have been. Magic is kinda like a sport. Things change and advance and people learn new strategies. A boxer from the 1800s isn't going to do the techniques one will now."

"So what's changed?" I asked.

"We just know more. We know more about physics, nature, psychology, and all the other sciences I can't name off the top of my head. Magic before had to fight against that, requiring more force from the user to do even the most basic spell. Now we know the work-around to find the path of least resistance."

"So work smarter not harder," I added.

"Yeah! It's no longer just imagining fire. It's about imagining the oxygen, the heat, and the matter fueling. The cause for the effect."

Tomas laid his hand flat against the table. He breathed in, closing his eyes on the out breath. The air felt thicker, the wind moving as new air moved into empty space that was pulled away. Wirelike red strands flickered to life. They drifted in the aether Tomas created and disappeared a few seconds after. A spark flashed over and over at the center of his hand, Tomas scrunching his face from psychological exertion. A flame erupted to life and engulfed Tomas's palm.

Tomas peeked at the flame with one eye but had to open the other to really believe it. He gasped out in a howling laugh.

"I did it!" Tomas exclaimed.

I matched his shock, my eyes transfixed on the magic fire.

"You did it!"

"I—Oh my goodness my hand is on fire!"

At first he tried smacking the fire away on the table. Instead of drowning out the fire, it left multiple inferno shaped handprints.

Tomas stood up. He reached for a cup of water but knocked it over by accident. Tomas ran around, looking for something to put it out. I finally processed the situation, guiding Tomas to one of the deep puddles close by. Tomas tripped forward and fell into the puddle. He plunged his hand into the water. Steam filled the area, beads of it collecting at our foreheads.

We were really lucky that day. The fire was weak, and the humidity kept it from getting any hotter. There are some pros to being a novice, and for Tomas it was being too inexperienced to make really bad mistakes.

As I wrapped Tomas's hand, I said "Maybe wear some gloves next time. I don't know if we can afford a hospital visit yet."

"Yet?" Tomas exclaimed.

"I'm joking… I hope."

On the second trip around the whole of Revival Fest, I began to notice more around me. New paths opened up. Streets appeared that hadn't existed before. New vendors and tents surfaced, each one more absurd than the last.

They started out small. Pixies dined in lanterns, their wings moving with the music's rhythm. A flock of them hovered around us, making the sound of wind chimes. The gnomes were more shy, preferring to watch us from the darkness. Except for Spudz, who sat atop a pole stealing people's jewelry with a magnetic fishing rod. I knew his name because I had to trade him the lollipop I got for the knife boomerang he stole from me.

Harpies sang to crowds of trolls and spriggans. Ghosts rolled by us, buying antiques they once owned. None of them knew my uncle, which both bothered and comforted me. It meant my uncle may have passed without any regrets, but it also meant there was less of a chance I could see him. Maybe Revival Fest would tell me, maybe they wouldn't. Either way, the world keeps turning.

Parading through Revival Fest, one thought appeared in the haze. Trellis was wrong. I wasn't my uncle and I wasn't who he thought I was. This night proved it. Yet, I left him thinking he was right about me. I needed to correct that.

Busting through his circus curtain entrance, I screamed at the top of my lungs for Trellis. He appeared like a cherub, descending down from the highest platform on a pair of miniature wings.

"Oh look, back for more questions I presume," Trellis said.

"No, I was just hoping to get that twinkle out of your eye," I said.

"Yeah! Woooooo!" Tomas shouted, working as my hype man.

Trellis giggled but stopped when his eyes met mine.

"Those eyes... Huh, you really did it. You see what I see. You didn't even need to cheat like your uncle. Color me impressed," Trellis said.

"I did, and it all makes sense now," I said.

"What does?" Trellis asked.

"It's you isn't it? The one keeping us from seeing Revival Fest ourselves," I said.

Trellis's confident exterior broke. He fell silent, his party eyes square on my own.

I was in a new state of being, a religious experience unfolding in front of me. I was a prophet, out to destroy heresy. In this new state, I saw Revival Fest for what it was. Secret rules weaved into its reality like a tapestry. Its first rule was to be free, but not at the cost of others.

"You thought you could call the shots right? Play us like a fiddle," I said.

"Weird for me to say this now, but what the heck are you talking about?" Tomas said.

"Think about it. We come for questions, and where do we get sent to? Trellis. What does he do once we grace his presence?" I got closer to Trellis "Sent us on a wild chase that he couldn't imagine us succeeding at. It could have worked too, if it weren't for me having such a good teacher."

Tomas sniffled on the verge of happy tears. "Damn straight."

Trellis's eyes moved to scan the crowd forming around us. He burst out laughing, one that felt as manufactured as the sandals he wore.

"Seems like the party animal isn't as secure as he said he was," I said.

Trellis stopped laughing, and said, "Right, like that makes any sense. Imagine that, Trellis, the party king of Revival Fest needing control over anything. 'Cause I don't. Whatever power I have now, happened upon me like anyone else. To say I ever would is a party foul in itself, and we don't play like that do we?"

I grinned. "You say that but look at you. You reek of desperation. You make this circus tent, have people drink your drinks, walk your walk and talk your talk. All the while you literally stand above us like some king. Sounds like you're making clowns out of us, and even worse, gatekeeping."

Everyone in the tent gasped, and the bartender fainted. Trellis gripped his fists, his chest puffing out like a bird.

I wasn't afraid. Fighting me would be a party foul and destroy any credibility he had with the crowd and Revival Fest itself. A fight was out of the question. Party games on the other hand were fair play, and anything could be a party game with some rules.

"We gonna do this or not?" Trellis said.

"Since it's your home turf, I'll let you pick the game," I said.

Trellis smiled, "Let's revisit the classics."

Trellis snapped his fingers. On his cue, the ground began to shake. Platforms broke and shifted across the circus like puzzle pieces. Metal stilts moved to support two new superstructures. These superstructures stood far from each other on opposite sides of this cathedral of a tent. Metal slabs sat diagonally, a massive hole in their center. Behind these metal slabs were platforms, catapults placed atop them.

"Ever heard of Cornhole? 'Cause I'll do you one better. Super Cornhole!" Trellis announced.

"We accept," I said.

"We? I mean yeah! We!" Tomas said.

Walking up the platform stairs, Tomas asked me, "Got any plans for this one?"

"Nope. You said it yourself. It's about the here and now."

"I don't know whether to feel proud or scared," Tomas said.

Cheering erupted as we made our way up. Monsters and humans roared out, their arms aimed for the stars. Steel bleachers drummed at by feet of varying shapes and sizes.

At the top was a catapult made from the same material as the platforms themselves. The siege work was a multi-man job, requiring a whole team to both aim and fire. Surrounding the catapult were red bean bag chairs, our ammo.

Getting to the edge, I shouted to Trellis. "What are the rules?"

"The rules are simple, first to three points wins. Anything that stays on the board is one point. Anything that falls through the center hole has three points." Trellis yelled.

With those rules, anyone lucky enough could win the game in the first turn. I discarded those thoughts. Filled to the top with liquid courage, I felt confident I could win the second it got to us.

A jumbotron was lowered down, showing a quarter.

"Heads, I'll go first. Tails, you'll go first," Trellis said.

The coin spun, blurring in the dark void. It slowed, wobbling over to one side. It landed heads. Trellis pumped his fist in the air, running over to his catapult to get to work.

"Well, that's not good," Tomas said.

"What're ya talking about? No way he'll hit us first turn," I said.

Trellis launched his beanbag. A blue comet soared in the air and dove onto the metal board. The platform shook as the beanbag compressed, sliding only a few feet from where it landed. Tomas and I leaned over to see. It wasn't going anywhere. One point for Trellis.

"Crap," I said.

Tomas ran to the back of the catapult, where a gear system was used to turn the entire siege work. He pushed at the turning bar, his feet sliding under him. The catapult lurched around, inching to face the metal board across from us.

As he did, I ran to the wheel used to control the distance the catapult would fire. Spinning the wheel, tension began to build as the restraining rope pulled at the catapult's arm. The crosshair above the wheel centered on the hole.

"Now!" I yelled.

Matilda tackled the activation lever. The catapult fired, a red bean bag chair careening towards the enemy's steel board. Streaking through the sky, the beanbag flew over the board and into the tent's fabric walls. No point for us. Turns out firing beanbag chairs was a lot harder than it looked.

It was now Trellis's turn. The first thing Trellis did was set up a lawn chair and let his lackeys do the work instead. His catapult fired and missed. Trellis shrugged, a smug smile decorating his lips. That bum knew what he was doing. He was showing off.

Tomas and I rushed to our positions, getting ready to send another volley. Just before I could adjust the wheel, one of Trellis's minions appeared and kicked me to the ground. I looked around, a group of leatherbound men surrounding me.

"Hey, that's… you know what? Screw it. Matilda!" I yelled.

Matilda leapt in the air, latching onto the head of one of the minions. With the henchmen distracted, I threw my cape over the two henchmen trying to pull Matilda off Henchman One. As they attempted to throw the heavy cape off, I ran and dropkicked them off the platform.

"Warlock Hunter!" I cheered.

"Oh my god, did you just kill them?" Tomas gasped.

"No time to think about moral implications, it's party time," I said.

"What have I created?" Tomas lamented.

Henchman One threw Matilda to the side, running to the lever in a mad dash to launch our catapult before we had fully aimed.

His hand extended out when Tomas said, "High five."

Tomas high fived the man. As he did, Hench One's palm combusted into flame. Screeching, the man flailed his arm to put the fire out. Running around the platform in pain, the henchmen tripped off the platform and down to the floor below.

We looked down to see if he was okay, only to see even more henchmen climbing up to get us. They swarmed up like bees to a hive.

"If you don't sober up with a plan, we'll be tasting more leather than a flogging convention," Tomas said.

I marched over to the catapult, where my Loot Box was. "Quit with them false dichotomies and follow my lead."

"Did you just pull a fallacy on me?" Tomas said.

"And I'll pull more if you don't get over here," I said back.

Tomas sighed, running over to help me. Ready to spring our plan, we waited for all the henches to be up and on their feet. What the henches saw was Tomas reclined on the ground, the boombox hiding half of his body.

"Hope you like remixed classics, idiots," Tomas said, sliding in the best Christian hip hop 2002 had to offer.

The music exploded to life, a deluge of youth pastors singing their hearts out to the most rhythmless music known to man. Choirs sang and moralized, raining down fire and brimstone. Don't drink, do drugs, or have premarital sex. Do all that and love god while doing it. It was torture to a hedonist's ears.

The henchmen grabbed their ears and cried out for it to stop. A few even fell to the ground, spinning in place attempting to run away. Tomas went to work with his warlock broom, one by one knocking the henches off the platform.

I got back to the wheel, turning it to aim. I stopped, realizing something. All these attempts I'd been using the crosshairs to aim. Yet that isn't the Revival Fest way. I needed to live on the edge and follow my instincts instead. I closed my eyes, turning it till my nerves told me to stop.

I opened my eyes and called for Matilda to fire. Nothing happened, she was too busy with the henches. I got up to walk to the lever when the Christian hip hop ended suddenly. The boombox was destroyed, a rock busting into it at the speed of sound. I swung around to see where it came from. Trellis waved to me in the far distance, a slingshot in his hand.

The henchmen sprung back to life, tackling Tomas and Matilda. I ran for the lever but was grabbed before I could reach it. Dragged by my legs away from the lever, I grabbed one last item from the bag. The henchmen piled onto me, making sure no part of me escaped. They held down every one of my limbs, except the one holding the knife boomerang.

I threw it, the boomerang spinning straight towards the restraining rope. It was sliced in half, causing the arm to activate. The bean bag launched, a shooting star arching in the air. It fell down, everyone freezing to see where it would land. The bag made a loud satisfying thunk as it landed straight through Trellis's hole.

Trellis and every single one of his henchmen's jaws dropped. Trellis sat up in his lawn chair, all smugness giving way for complete shock. The henchmen got up from the pile, freeing us.

Tomas, Matilda and I ran to each other for a massive group hug. We cheered, jumping up and down. The crowd chanted our names, pacifiers and glow sticks thrown our way. Breaking from our group hug, we all started to dance. Trellis stormed off. High from victory, I wasn't able to notice the boombox. Tripping on it, I tumbled backwards and off the platform.

I fell, my arm outstretched. The world around me turned dark, my hand remaining visible. I was in a state of freefall. My mind was now in constant and ever present dreaming. Peace cooled my mind, disposing of panic. In this soundless world, I could think and feel in a way I couldn't before. I was more than I had ever been before. I won the reality lottery and was relishing in it.

"You did well," a voice echoed in my ear.

"Huh, I did," I said.

"You must have a lot of questions, don't you?"

I smiled. It was right, I did have a lot of questions. Yet, at that moment of pure bliss, I wanted to ask none of them.

# CHAPTER 12

Ever entered a room and then forgot the reason why? That's what this space was like. Every second and minute that passed by in that darkness was a space of temporary amnesia. In this meditative state, thoughts came and went like the wind.

As time passed, the space began to change, cooling and warming with the heat of my soul. Paint strokes smeared across my vision in waves. Various chroma rippled and changed to my breathing rhythm.

"Would you like a second? I'm sure this feels overwhelming," Revival Fest said, its voice soothing to both the mind and heart.

"Bit of an understatement," I said.

Revival Fest laughed. "It is. Though I'm afraid we can't afford to give you a second to adjust, due to you needing to put a stop to a certain someone's plans. Instead, I'll ask all the questions you had ready in your head before encountering me. Which I have access to, you being in my domain and all."

"I'm listening," I said.

"So what am I? Well I'm the combined psyche of all people who have and had entered what you call Revival Fest. How so? It's simple, actually. It's the same way magic and other supernatural occurrences are made. Life did as life does and dreamt of more than what could be seen. Life is the key to it all, even necromancy, which is life lying to itself. It's all a bit nebulous," it said.

I nodded, wrapping my brain around the concept as best I could, using the physical as reference. "No, I think I get it. It's like waves on a rocky shore. They mold and change the rocks, which life can do the same in a more metaphysical way. All it needs is time."

"Wow, you're good. In another time, you could have been one of my greatest representatives," it continued. "Now for the big question. What is Percival Maelie planning for Revival Fest? What I can tell you for sure is that he is in no way able to act against me. What he is after instead is information, the kind he could get from one vendor by the alias of Karl Christen. He's a thief, his main talent being fencing off valuable supernatural items in areas like Revival Fest. You actually encountered him before, he was the robed man who sold Tomas a magic book. And yes, that was also stolen."

"Crap," I said.

"If you hurry, you can intercept him and stop any plans he has."

I began to lower, the color again disappearing back into darkness.

"Wait!" I shouted.

My descent stopped.

"Why help me? Why choose me?" I asked.

"Because you're a quiet and kind soul who went out of their way to play on my terms in the greatest way possible. If there is anyone I can trust to defend us in our greatest time of need, it would Jonathan Whitlock and Tomas Seer. Expect to hear my call again. I'm counting on you."

I closed my eyes. Opening them, I found myself laying on the circus floor, unharmed. Everyone surrounded me, Tomas and Matilda at the forefront.

Wiping at his eyes, Tomas said "Holy crap, you had me worried."

I sat up, asking, "Is everyone else who fell okay?"

"Yeah, don't know how, some of them fell off worse than you did," Tomas said.

"Revival Fest works in mysterious ways," I said.

"What?" Tomas said, confused.

I leapt back to my feet. "I know where Percival is going, if we hurry we can catch him."

"You do? How?" Tomas asked.

"Revival Fest told me, I'll explain later," I said.

I ran out of the Circus, Tomas and Matilda close behind.

Revival Fest had become second nature to me. Every corridor was mapped into my deepest gray matter. My brain became a GPS exclusively for Revival Fest. Making my way through crowds of partygoers, I vaulted over churro carts and spun around street jugglers.

The vendor was down south, close to the middle. If Percival wanted an easy escape, his best chance would be the main entrance. That would be out of the way from where he was going. In a game of cat and mouse, I had the advantage.

Getting to the vendor, I busted through the curtains ready for a fight. Instead I was instantly blinded by a handful of sand. I fell to the ground, digging at my eyes.

"I'd say it's a shock to see you Mr. Whitlock, if I hadn't paid good money for this very moment," Percival said as he strolled past me.

"My eyes," I said, unable to give a clever response.

After he exited, Tomas and Matilda entered.

"You okay? What happened?" Tomas said, helping me up from the ground.

"It's whatever, just chase him," I said.

We chased Percival. No matter what Tomas and I did, we couldn't catch up to him. He looked like he wasn't even running. What made it even more confusing was that he was going deeper into Revival Fest rather than trying the entrance like I expected.

We were about to corner him, when Percival decided to turn into what was a dead end. When we caught up, he was nowhere to be found.

"How in the hell?" Tomas pointed to Percival

He was running atop the solid roofs lining the Revival Fest's border.

I ran to a group of crates. Using them as makeshift steps, I rushed up to the tiled roofing and after Percival. I was alone now. Tomas struggled to keep up. He was still climbing up by the time I got near Percival.

Sprinting close behind, I waited for the right time to tackle and restrain him. Before I had a chance, Percival swung around and threw his very own knife boomerang. I ducked to avoid the spinning blade, taking a quick look to see if the thing would hit anyone behind me.

I grabbed two of my daggers in response, and threw them at Percival. He pulled a portable shield from his cloak and deflected them.

"What even?" I stammered.

"I'm shocked you didn't put it together sooner. You really think I would do this alone without hedging my bets," Percival said.

A sudden realization hit me "No,"

I wasn't that old hag's only customer. Percival also gave her a visit. This was double trouble since he had the wisdom to actually use his fortune properly.

Percival stopped after hitting an area he couldn't climb like before. He turned around slowly with the smug smile he usually had.

I was out of breath. My body had been either dancing or running the entire night. Even the total concentration awarded to me by Revival Fest was nothing in comparison to the absolute strain my body felt.

I let out the words. "It's over... heh... this is the last—"

Percival interrupted me, and said, "Grappling hook."

He pointed a massive grappling gun in the air, firing a cable-tied hook into the tree branches. A powerful engine in the gun revved, pulling him up to higher ground.

"What is this? The fortune hag playing favorites?" I yelled.

"Don't take this personally, Mr. Whitlock. Some just have a better time with fate," Percival said.

Hitting the peak of Revival Fest's wood palisade, Percival turned to face me. He gave a small salute and went over to the other side of the wall.

I stood there, the whole situation hitting me in one big wave. I fell to my feet. I had spent all my luck, and there was nothing else to give. Consumed by doom and gloom, I barely noticed when Tomas and Matilda had caught up with me.

Tomas was more out of breath than I was. "Holy crap, dude… you guys ran… I need to exercise… heh."

The adrenaline settled, my ringing nerves giving way to silence. I tried to get up, but gave up as I did, choosing to just sit back down. I reclined, my arms propping me up.

We stayed there for a bit, the wind cooling us.

"I'm sorry, man," Tomas said. "If we hadn't gotten so deep into it, we would have been able to get him."

"It's okay," I said.

"It is?"

"Yeah," I said, getting up and brushing myself off. "We might not have stopped him today, but there's always tomorrow. We did what we could now. All there is to do is to move on and be ready for whatever comes next."

Tomas looked a bit shocked at how I was taking the whole situation, responding, "Huh, I guess it is getting late."

"I'll drive, I think Revival Fest sobered me up," I said.

"Yeah, I'm gonna need an explanation on how the heck that works," Tomas said.

As we left, I explained the best I could what I had seen and experienced at Revival Fest. He listened, but understandably struggled to understand anything I was talking about. There were a lot of questions. I was fine with it. It's about time I answered questions instead of asking them.

Revival Fest is beyond anything I had and maybe will ever see. As mysterious as the forests surrounding them, it's a place of freedom that revels in secrets. It's neither a good nor evil place, managing to avoid any moral definition. Leaving it, I realized I needed it more than I thought I would. Maybe the reason no one wants to talk about Revival Fest, is because they don't want to admit ever needing something like it. Whatever it is, I'm glad I

went.

# CHAPTER 13

When competing for crowds, lies are what win out. That's how it felt playing guard dog for the grand opening of the Helford Mafia History Museum. It was a momentous occasion, great for both tourism and the photo booth. Everything needed to be perfect, so we were hired to keep the town's weirdness at an all-time low while it went down.

I wasn't expecting much, since the paranormal isn't exactly attracted by the allure of cutting red ribbons. Tomas and I chose to watch from a distance. I sat with a pair of shades. My equipment was ready to go at a moment's notice. We just needed to act busy, and we'd get an easy few hundred to add to the savings. I did waste some money making a few incomplete salt circles to help sell the idea we were doing anything important.

Tomas, on the other hand, wasn't taking it easy. He'd been annoyed since we got the job. He leaned against a tree with his arms crossed. I decided to give him some time to cool before asking what was wrong.

Harriet's speech started out well. She stood at the entrance with a speaker and podium. A projector behind her flashed images of the soon-to-be museum. It presented Tommy guns, old stock cars, and three-piece suits. Wax mobsters gave cinematic poses in glass displays. Their faces scowled, teeth clamped down on cigars.

"They really went all out. Can see each individual wrinkle on them," I said.

"This is so stupid," Tomas said.

"How so?" I asked.

"It's a waste of time. Our town never even had a speakeasy. Much less the freaking mob." Tomas gestured at the mannequins.

"Hm, what do you think they'll put in there?" I asked.

Tomas shrugged. "I don't know. The only thing I can think of is this shed that one guy used to hide alcohol. It'll fit in, since there won't be anything else to show off."

Wrapping up her speech, Harriet said, "I'd like to thank everyone for coming here to celebrate Helford's colorful history."

"Colorful!" Tomas protested at the top of his lungs.

Everyone turned and looked at us. Harriet's displeasure could be seen states over.

"Oh crap," I sighed.

"This stuff is beige at best." Tomas walked toward the crowd. "And it isn't our history."

Harriet eked out an uncomfortable laugh "Helford's a small town, one that's thankfully been quiet for a very long time. Places like here never have a large pool when it comes to history. Just think of what it'll do for our small community."

"Do what? Lie to everyone? We have probably the most interesting history around. Secret societies have been visiting here since this place was settled. You could make five museums with all the occult stuff we have laying around," Tomas announced to everyone.

"I'm sure I could speak for everyone when I say that none of that would be in the best interest of the town. No one wants to be the town known for freakish oddities. Besides, those were just rumors. Old wives' tales to pass the time and keep children out of the woods," she said, more so towards the audience than to Tomas.

The crowd's mood deteriorated. They weren't happy, but not in a vitriolic sense. They were tired of Tomas. Exhausted over one outburst too many. If there was any rage before, it had been spent a long time ago. Tomas's composure cracked under the sea of apathetic annoyance.

"That's a lie and you know it. If it wasn't, your brother's house wouldn't be a crater—" I snuck behind Tomas and pulled him away before he could say anything more.

"And we're done! Happy grand opening, everyone!"

Out of earshot, I said "Dude, what are you doing?"

"Don't you 'dude' me, why didn't you back me up?" Tomas said.

"Because we're being paid not to cause a scene, and we can't jeopardize that," I explained.

"Oh, real rich coming from the guy who turned down twelve grand," Tomas snapped back.

"That was for ethical reasons," I said.

"And what I'm doing isn't? We've helped this town in so many ways, and this is how they repay us? By acting like we don't exist?" Tomas said.

I sighed, trying not to get upset. "Look, it happened, and there's nothing else we can do about it now. Harriet is right, even if she's lying. We don't have any real proof of ancient orders kicking it in Helford. So for this moment, we just have to bite our tongues and let the politician have her way."

Tomas frowned, his eyes looking away from my own. Things started going on in his head, some weighing of his decisions. When he was done, he marched off towards the car.

"Where are you going now?" I asked.

"I'm going to the house. If anyone had evidence of secret societies in Helford, it was your uncle," he said.

He wasn't crazy to think that, with all the strange things my uncle had collected. The part that made him crazy was storming off to look for it now. I paced after him. Unreasonable or not, I wasn't going to let him do it on his own.

We were about to get in the car when a familiar surly voice stopped us.

"Where are you two going?" he said

"Sheriff," Tomas and I said, nodding.

Sheriff Hush was a tall man. Despite that, he had the unpleasant ability to sneak up on anyone he didn't like. He had a handlebar mustache, and shades that he wore both day and night. His thumbs were tucked into his waistband, his mouth chewing on hell-knows-what.

"You think you can go ahead and disturb the peace of this town and expect to get away with it?" Hush said.

Tomas and Hush have had problems with each other since before I moved to Helford. The hatred between them was one-sided, Hush always seeming to be the one who wanted to start things.

"People have a right to express their opinions, Hush." Tomas said.

"And where does it say you can interrupt a town-sponsored event?" Hush said.

"You tell me, you're the one always telling me to read the constitution." Tomas said back.

Getting the sense that Tomas might get arrested real soon, I said, "No need to worry about us, Sheriff. We're not planning to disturb the event any more than we already have."

My face reflected back at me as Hush watched me. He pointed at me, asking Tomas.
"Does he speak for you, Thomas?"

Tomas closed his eyes and took in a deep breath.
"He does."

Chewing for an extra second, Hush said, "Then I'll leave you to it. Don't have me catch you acting up again."

He finally left us alone doing the prison warden stroll.

I felt guilty, like I should have said more. Tomas looked put down one time too many. His expression adrift in a sea of listlessness.

"Tomas, I'm… I'm sorry, man," I said.

"It's okay, there was nothing you could do," he said.

Driving back home, that feeling stayed.

The first place we looked for evidence was my uncle's basement. Boxes full of strange supernatural items lined the shelves. Any occult item Uncle Whitty found, no matter its danger or worth, he kept down here. Something was bound to be in one of them.

Things didn't seem fruitful. We opened every box and cataloged the items. Haunted doll houses and sacred tomes. Vampire teeth necklaces and a jar of werewolf eyes. Matilda helped some but ended up distracted with the haunted doll house. Each box of magic junk brought Tomas to a new low. We held our breath at the last box. It could have been everything or nothing.

We opened the box. It was a single joke book.

"What?" Tomas grabbed the joke book, rolling through the pages "There has to be something to it."

Tomas read through one of the pages. He started laughing. The kind I never heard from him. He gasped over and over for air, tears in his eyes. In a split second he threw the book against the wall and screamed in frustration.

"Laugh? He kept a magic book that makes you laugh? Where did he even get it?" Tomas said.

He cupped his face with his hands. His laughing tears mixed with those made from dejection. We both sat crisscross on the floor, surrounded by unloaded boxes. Matilda dropped a ball and ran after it under the shelves. Tomas held onto his legs, forming himself into a ball. He stared straight ahead, eyes a tired red. I crawled closer to him.

"Is this really about proving Harriet wrong?" I asked.

The air went still, and Tomas said, "Have you ever lived somewhere where no one saw you as normal?"

"I can't say I have," I said.

"I was always that kind of person… Everyone would look at me like I did something wrong. It hurts knowing that the things I love are the same things people see as something to hide away. Imagine that, your life being so taboo that it can only be done at the dead of night or at Revival Fest… I wanted to show them that I was worth more than just a holiday. That I was worth every day of the week. That I was more a piece of this town's history than a booze shed."

I listened to every word. I placed my hand on his shoulder.

"You're worth a lot to me Tomas," I said.

The tension in his body lessened. He smiled. His hand wrapped around mine.

Waddling over to us, Matilda presented us with a small wood box. Tomas grabbed it, looking over every corner of it.

He opened it. Pressed in a green silk cast, was an ornate coin. The coin presented a grouping of mountains, a crosshair shaped hole at the center of the coin. "The Down Nose Society" read on the top. The bottom was a set of numbers.

Tomas pointed at the mountains "Wait a second, I know those mountains. They're the Dylan Mountains."

"If that's real, could that cross be marking—" I stopped, both Tomas and I turning to look at each other.

"We did it!" Tomas exclaimed.

We jumped back to standing. Tomas picked up Matilda, twirling around to celebrate his eureka moment.

"Thank you," Tomas said over and over to Matilda. When Tomas realized who he was spinning around with, he placed Matilda back on the ground. He cleared his throat and said, "Thank you, I really appreciated that."

Matilda hugged him and he relented.

"But how are we going to know where to go? The side of a few mountains isn't exactly a good map," I asked.

Tomas gave a clever grin. "What do you think the numbers at the bottom are?"

My face began to match Tomas's. "You're two steps ahead of me."

"With a partner like you. You learn some things," Tomas answered.

We got ready for a trip to the Dipperty-Mabel Forests. It was time to find ourselves a secret society.

# CHAPTER 14

Witnessing that landscape, the only thing I could think of was how green everything was. It surrounded us. Green leaves caught and weaved soft mist to water droplets. Slipping out the leaves' grasp, the water smacked against our rain jackets like darts against a board.

The same thing could be said about the mist itself. The haze rolled over us and down the mountain peak. The peak was as subdued as the mist that surrounded it, the plants finding no issue claiming it as their own.

It was the perfect scene for hiking, which was what made it so easy to drive here in the first place. Disturbing this peak was the beginning of a prominent nature trail. Benches, bathrooms, and a vending machine, the basic necessities for human survival. Passing the edge of the parking lot, one question came up in our minds. Why here? Why hide a secret society in an area where people would be out looking for things?

"Are you sure this is the right place?" I asked Tomas.

Tomas stood close to the peak, searching the area with my uncle's birdwatching binoculars.

"It has to be. We just have to keep looking," Tomas said.

"I don't know, I just wasn't expecting this place to have a gift shop," I said.

Sitting at the bench, I gave myself time to take in the area's own system of things. I noticed the display that was set up close to the bench. On it was basic information about the area, including the ecosystem's origins, animals, and history of the nature trail. Skimming over it, my eyes caught something interesting.

"The nature trail was officially founded in the two thousands," I said.

"Maybe the secret society moved spots before all this stuff was built," Tomas remarked.

"'Officially' is what's getting to me. Doesn't that mean people were traveling this area before the roads here were built? If that's true, and the society was set up here before that, wouldn't people have found evidence of them by now?" I said.

"Something here is missing, I can feel it," Tomas said, his eyes still on the binoculars.

I went over to Tomas, standing beside him to take a peek at everything below us. The birds played their melodies, the trees and crickets working as percussion. Vast gray skies turned the greens more muted. Given the chance, I would have trekked this land for all its secrets.

"This really is something isn't it?" I said.

"Never took you as a nature guy," Tomas said.

"I don't share that part of me to a lot of people. Most look at you weird when you say you could go days without seeing another person's face," I said.

"I think it's nice," Tomas said.

Something about that made me feel warm inside. Taking in that warmth, I noticed something.

"Isn't that the same mountain shown on the coin?" I asked, pointing it out to Tomas.

Zeroing in with the binoculars, Tomas said "It is."

I pulled out the coin and held it out so that it aligned with the mountain. Through the crisscrossed hole, hidden away by the trees, was a small alcove in the rock. I tapped Tomas's shoulder to get his attention.

"That over there, what do you see with the binoculars?"

"I don't see…" he said, his words drifting off as he looked further. "Wait, I see something."

We both got excited.

"What is it?" I asked.

Tomas handed me the binoculars. "See for yourself."

My vision blurred, my eyes attempting to focus on the mass of details. As my sight cleared, a small thin line over the treetops appeared.

"That's… that's a cable!" I exclaimed.

"If we can follow that cable up the mountain, we can find the main location of this secret society," Tomas said.

"We found it, we really found it," I said.

"So, how do you feel about going on a short nature hike with me?" Tomas said, a smile forming on his lips.

I smiled back. "I thought you'd never ask."

Diverging from the trail, we made our way through the valley to the mountain. Our legs grew tired, wading through shallow creeks and fallen trees. We kept track of where we went using maps and compasses. Better to be prepared than to be lost.

The farther we got, the less we saw of civilization. No more plastic trash or marked trees appeared in our periphery. The fresh air kept us going. In and out the world spun. New complexities taking over the ones we felt before.

We made it to the base of the mountain, aiming for around where the cable would be. Squinting our eyes to see past the trees, we saw a small wooden house. Behind the house were the metal cables. They were much thicker closer up, measuring more than the width of my arm. Suspended on that cable was a cable car. The inside looked to fit twelve people, the elements having chipped away what was once an opulent interior.

Inside the house was a massive engine, designed to move the car up and down the mountain. Rust had eaten at the gears, along with my confidence of it still being able to work. Not wanting to end our journey at that, Tomas poured in a gas tank left close by.

The engine sprang into action. We peered out, and saw the train car beginning to move. I ran into the car without a second thought. Tomas hesitated and was forced to chase after the car before it ascended out of reach. Tomas jumped and grabbed onto the edge of the doorway. I pulled him up, using all the strength I had to get him inside.

Now in the car, we let out exhausted breaths. It rivaled our first meeting with Basket Case as one of the stupidest things we had ever done. A lot of faith went into two old metal cables and an engine.

Three small metal towers worked to hold the cable up. I did everything that I could to tell myself that the aching groans they made as we passed them were my imagination. A log cabin formed into our view through the dense fog. Inside it was the other engine used for the cable car.

We jumped off as soon as we were close to it.

I'd never been so happy to have fallen face first into solid ground. Looking around us, we found ourselves inside a strange alcove in the mountain. Trees shrouded it from the outside world, making it impossible to be seen from a distance.

Plant life had taken back what was left of the area. Grass grew to knee height, and vines covered what the other plants couldn't. Parting the grass revealed a small stone trail which led further into the alcove. With little else to go on, we followed the trail.

The trail ended at a moss covered boulder. Behind that was what remained of the secret society we tried so hard to look for. A manor, made from a combination of brick and stone, had collapsed in on itself from what seemed to be a fire.

Tomas went to investigate the house while I fixated on the massive boulder. It seemed out of place to the rest of the area, like it was moved here. A thick layer of moss covered the stone.

Wiping away the moss revealed the words "Here be the home of the Down Nose Society. A world unto its own."

Underneath that phrase was an abstract carving of the world. A hand ready to bear down on it like a bird of prey. I took a picture for further research.

When I was done, I went over to Tomas. He stood in what remained of the meeting room. The floors were charred black. Wood broken in stark angles. The only thing left truly intact was the stone chimney at the edge of the manor.

Tomas wandered over to the destroyed table, now turned to charcoal. He knelt down, picking up a coin from the black remains. It was the same kind of coin found hidden away in my uncle's basement.

No single emotion showed on his face. Instead it was a mix of many. Confusion, sadness, regret, and frustration all showed in clear view. His thumb ran across the grooves of the coin.

"What happened to them?" Tomas said.

"I don't know. It could have been anything. An accident. An act of passion. Even something premeditated. It could have been anyone, too," I said.

He seemed on the brink of tears. He tried to look up to hold them back.

"All this work... just to find a burnt heap left on a mountain," he let out.

I looked for anything to comfort him. "I don't see any remains. Maybe if we go out and do some more research we can—"

"Do what? This all over again?" Tomas said.

"I'm just trying to find a silver lining in all of this," I said.

"I don't want a silver lining…" Tomas wiped his face. "I don't want to plan… I just want to be here."

At that moment, I saw what Tomas needed most. Approaching him, I turned him to face me, and wrapped my arms tight around him. His head pressed deep in my shoulder, tears running off like rain. I held his head in one arm and his back with the other.

"It'll be okay," I said over and over.

"I'm so sorry. I wasted your time, with nothing to show you. We… we—" Tomas struggled to talk.

"We did what we needed to, okay? Don't be sorry about that. You are what you are, whether through thick or thin, you are you. There are no words to describe how great something like that is," I said. "It'll be alright. We'll be alright."

# CHAPTER 15

The air was so fresh up there. Cold yet welcoming, the wind cooled my tired muscles. I sat down with Tomas at the entrance of the destroyed manor. We existed amongst a fading memory. A place of nowhere. That's the thing about abandoned places, they continue to breathe even as we leave them.

Since crying, Tomas had gone quiet. It was strange to see him like that. When I first met him, I thought you'd have to be confident verging on arrogance to be the way he was. Here I was now seeing the full picture of him. Tomas would fight all of Helford just to be what he wanted to be but continued to carry the same anxieties of fitting in that everyone else had.

I had felt similar things, except in reverse. I wanted to be so much more than people expected of me. I wanted to be irreplaceable. Something that I could be as an occult investigator. Few could do what I could do now, and I was more than happy to have that spot in life. In that way, I also wanted to prove people wrong.

Thinking of that, I asked Tomas "What made you want to go with me?"

We sat for a minute before Tomas said, "'Cause you listened to me… and you helped me when others would have just laughed at me. It made me want to see it through. To know what it was like to be around someone who respected the fact I was human."

"That does make me realize something," I said.

"What?"

"I don't think I could have gone through any of our adventures without your help," I said.

Tomas smiled, resting his head against his knees.

"This really is beautiful isn't it?" he said.

"Yeah," I said, leaning my back against the stair.

"Fun too," Tomas said.

"It was," I responded.

The moment was ruined by a cold shiver running up my spine. Something was watching us. I put one arm up to guard Tomas, the other hovered over my holster.

"Scatter," I shouted to Tomas, pushing him away from me.

We both rolled away as a green blur flew by us. Claws the size of my torso raked at the area Tomas had been a second before. Due to momentum, the creature continued its forward leap. It dragged itself to a halt using its own claws.

It looked like an upright monitor lizard. It hunched low in a predator's stance. Its arms extended from its shoulders down to its legs. Yellow eyes bulged from the side of its head, black circles rippling from a slit-thin pupil.

Still on the ground, I pulled out the Final Line, and emptied the gun into the creature. The bullets made their mark, yet each one bounced off his armored chest. None of them broke skin, leaving only deep purple bruises. The creature came towards me.

It was faster than anything we encountered before. It glided like wind through blades of grass. Basket Case and Trellis always had something slowing them down, distracting them. This thing had one goal in mind, and it was seeing me chopped and diced.

It leapt at me on the last step, both arms pointed above its head. I pushed myself up and attempted to backstep away. I was too slow. Claws swept down and sliced an X-shaped wound into my chest. Blood spat out, the meat under my skin now open for me to see and feel.

My hand clenched at the newly-made loose flap on my shirt. Warm blood stuck to anything it touched, my palm included. My heartbeat sounded the alarms in my ear. Each breath ached in my lungs.

Smelling my fear, the monster made another attack. Lifting its body with both arms, it kicked me square where it last wounded me. The air was knocked out of me. I rolled across the cold wet grass, ten whole yards away.

The breathing pains weren't an issue now, because I couldn't breathe either way. My mouth tried to gulp in some air but couldn't. It was like I forgot how to be alive. Up was down and down was up. I laid on my stomach like a newborn. My vision blurred with straining tears.

The monster gave a reptilian stare. It held little malice in its eyes, a telltale sign of an experienced killer. It got low to start running, claws ready to tear me to ribbons.

"Hey!" Tomas boomed.

The creature stopped, its attention now on Tomas. He stared down the lizard, eyes never leaving their mark.

Tomas pulled out thick work gloves, strange markings burned into both of them.

Pulling on the gloves, Tomas said, "You're looking chilly. How about I turn up the heat?"

Tomas held out his arm. Moths, gnats, and other bugs in the air around the lizard burst into flames. Heat distorted the light around it. The creature soon realized the danger it was under. The monster hissed, its body receding in pain. Moisture in its body sizzled off in heaps of steam.

It looked around for a way to end its suffering. It shot a look my way and barreled towards me. The spell followed the creature, burning anything in its wake. If it wanted to get Tomas to end his own spell, then getting me hurt with it would do the trick.

"Think you're slick? Here!" Tomas shouted.

Tomas clenched his gloved fist, causing a magical cavalcade of cause and effect. One of the remaining stone walls of the manor began to crack in the middle. Buckling from the newfound lack of support, the wall twisted and fell onto the creature. Flattened by tested stone, the creature was stopped dead in its tracks by a pile of rubble.

With a sneaking suspicion that it wasn't fully down for the count, I stumbled past the stone pile over to Tomas.

"Field trip's over, let's get out before it does," I said.

"Right with you," Tomas said.

We sprinted down the stone trail over to the log cabin. I was struggling behind Tomas, slowed by my new injuries. Busting down the door, we ran around the engine to see if any cable cars were on our side. There were none.

"We're dead if there isn't a car soon," I said.

"There's one traveling up," Tomas said, pointing.

I looked out the window. "How long before that?"

"I don't know, a minute maybe," Tomas said as he looked through the mist at the cable car.

"We don't have that time," I said.

"You don't think I know that?" Tomas said.

The lizard came into view, running at full speed towards the cabin. I reloaded my revolver.

"You got anything with ice?" I asked Tomas.

"In a pinch, yeah," Tomas responded.

"Let's see how Mr. Cold-Blooded does with freezing," I said.

I aimed my revolver, and said, "On my mark."

Tomas extended his arm, steady. We needed perfect precision for it to work, but my hand was shaking from the pain. We waited, letting the lizard get closer and closer to the cabin.

Just when the cable car entered the cabin, I yelled "Now!"

Tomas did his thing, the air turning cold around the lizard. Small ice crystals formed, fell, and shattered on the ground. The lizard's breath became visible. As the cold air enveloped it, the lizard's skin turned dry and rigid.

I did my part, firing three bullets into the monster. Its skin now brittle, the bullets shattered through and lodged into the creature's flesh. The creature yelped, grabbing at its chest from the now open wounds.

A main downside of the cold would be that its wounds would bleed less. It didn't matter though, since my main goal was to buy time.

"Hurry," I said to Tomas.

The cable car made its turn to go down the mountain. We hopped on just before it left the cabin. We slumped down onto the chairs as we got more distant from the creature.

Just before the first metal tower, I said, "We're gonna need to prepare for things like this."

Tomas was about to respond when his eyes widened in shock. He pointed towards the cabin above us.

"I don't think we're out just yet," he said.

I followed Tomas's hand. The lizard stood at the edge where the cable cars entered and left the cabin. It inspected the cable, grabbing it with one of his massive claws. Its eyes held a venomous determination. It lifted its legs, letting its weight slide it down the cable towards us. Like a zipline, it gained more speed the farther it went down the cable.

"How the hell are we going to fight that?" Tomas said.

"You tell me," I said.

The lizard slammed against the cable car. Metal bent inwards and the trolley swung back and forth. Tomas and I tumbled inside, broken glass flying our way. The lizard reached an arm into the car, intent on pulling us out kicking and squealing. We scrambled away from its sharp claws, ending up on one side.

Its arm got closer and closer, and we had less room to run. We were at the end of our ropes. I had no more plans. All I could do now was apologize.

"Tomas... I'm... I'm sorry I brought you into this. You wouldn't be dealing with this if it weren't for me," I said.

Tomas looked at me and scoffed. "You brought me into this? Nobody can ever bring me into anything. I chose to be here."

Tomas got up and approached the lizard.

"And there's no getting rid of me now."

Tomas stood his ground, defiant. I felt a twinge in the air and a creep up my spine. Tomas's own description of magic appeared in my mind. Anyone can feel magic, and I could feel him collect it by the gallons. It felt like determination in liquid form. It pooled around him and lifted into the air. Thin red strands flickered in the aether surrounding him.

Tomas yelled, the inside rattling at the sound. The lizard was thrown back by an invisible force. It held tight, claws carved into the metal skin. At the end of its strength, the monster was launched away like a leaf in the wind. Flying backwards, the monster crashed through the third metal tower.

The tower leaned forward, causing us to fall forward. Instead of the soft climb we had before, we were now rolling down at high speeds. The speed caused the wire to decouple with each tower we passed. We slipped down lower and lower, close enough to kiss the treetops. We shot down like a falling star and crashed into the house.

The car broke off its cable and went straight through the wall. The bottom slid on the moss covered forest floor, our bodies thrown around inside. When we stopped, we couldn't tell if we made it or crashed through the afterlife.

"You alive?" I asked Tomas.

Tomas groaned. "Unfortunately."

I strained myself and said, "Oh, you'll be alright."

"I know," Tomas responded.

Opening the door, we found ourselves at the end of a Tommy gun. It was the wax mobsters from the museum, graced with the miracle of life. There was only one person I knew who could do something like that.

"Jonathan Whitlock, interesting seeing you here," said Percival Maelie.

He appeared from behind the mobster army, guarded shoulder to shoulder by Scar Joe and Lucky Luciani. He had the smuggest look a human face could make. Tomas and I raised our hands in the air.

"Careful, you might cramp something grinning like that," I said.

"You'll have to forgive me, Mr. Whitlock. Because for once, I'm relieved to see you," he said.

"Why's that? You decided to help people for a change?" I said.

"Don't be silly. I'm relieved because you may have done all my work here for me. Which brings me to my first question. What did you find there, Mr. Whitlock?" Percival said.

"Nothing you'd find interesting," I answered.

A loud hissing roar echoed from somewhere on the mountain.

"From the looks of it, Mr. Whitlock, this back and forth will do you more harm than it does me," Percival said.

"What? Is that suit stab proof?" I asked.

"No, but I have a counter to it that you don't have. Which I'll happily use after it finishes tearing you apart. Working with me will be much less gruesome."

I had nothing to say. He was right. That thing would kill us at a moment's notice, and being held up made that fact inevitable.

"If we give you what we found, will you let us go?" Tomas asked.

"I see no reason for this to end in bloodshed," Percival answered.

"Then here." Tomas tossed over the coin from the manor.

Percival caught and inspected the coin. He gave a respectful nod. "A pleasure doing business with you, Tomas."

He walked into the forest with his retinue of wax mobsters. Where he went, I didn't know, we were too busy running to find out.

# CHAPTER 16

It was pitch black by the time we got back to the parking lot. Our arms were dragging behind us, our knuckles making full contact with the sidewalk. We were met by an unexpected bright light aimed straight at our faces. It was Deputy Cutty, Sheriff Hush's little helper.

"There you are. Where have you two been?" he said.

"Got sent here to look into some going-ons and got lost on the way," I said, pulling the sides of my jacket to hide the open wounds.

We'd been running off of adrenaline the whole trip back, and my own fear had worked me through my pain better than anything else.

"Better question, why are you here?" Tomas added.

"Oh," Cutty lowered his light. "Hush told me to follow you guys around. Said something about you two being up to no good. Either way I lost you guys hours ago, so good thing you didn't do anything while I wasn't around."

Tomas and I looked at each other and then at Helford's finest.

"Yep, totally," I said.

"Nothing weird is happening here," Tomas added.

Cutty squinted till his eyes were close to shut. He kept at his suspicious gaze, going from one person to the other. The intensity came to a sudden and warm conclusion.

The Deputy smiled, holstering his flashlight "Welp, I'll go ahead and leave you guys be. You two have a good night."

Once he was out of view, we ran to my beat up Corolla. We weren't risking another lizard attack. Blazing down the hill, we made sure there was a massive gap between us and the monster. We held our breath, keeping an eye out for anything that could fly in from the side of the road. Miles in, we finally allowed ourselves to breathe.

We both freaked out, expressing it in our own way. Tomas ran his mouth at the speed of one word a millisecond. He went off about how scary it was, how dangerous it was, and the craziest fact of all: we were still alive. I sat still, eyes wide, breathing.

This fight felt like a tougher pill to swallow when compared to the others we had before. Our last encounters were made on our terms. We knew what we were getting into and had the time to prepare for whatever came next.

This one was different. We came in not expecting to get ambushed and skewered. It was a wakeup call. Something like that lizard, with the same intent to kill, could appear when we least expected. Everywhere was dangerous until proven otherwise. That thought stuck with me for a long time.

When it felt like a safe distance, I asked Tomas if he felt okay.

"I think," he said, then added, "I'm sorry… for giving Percival the coin."

"We'll survive. It's not like we knew what it did," I said.

"What do you think he needed it for?" Tomas asked.

I shrugged. "All I can say is that it won't be good."

Tomas sighed. "It's so annoying, man. Why does he always have to be two steps ahead of us?"

"I don't think he is," I said.

"Why?"

"'Cause," I pulled out the coin my uncle had. "He didn't know about this."

"Of course he didn't, your uncle had it," Tomas said.

"But my uncle's house had been empty for weeks until I was handed the deed for it. He could have searched every inch of that house and found the coin before any of us knew what was up. Yet, he didn't. Instead he's going on this wild goose chase to get the same things that are held up in my basement."

"You think something's keeping him from going into the house?" Tomas suggested.

"It might be. We'll need to investigate the house. Get an idea of what might be going on."

When we did make it back home, the first thing we did was to dress my gaping wounds. The pain was setting in by then, and it took a lot longer for me to work through it to get some rest. Once I could, it was the best sleep I got in ages. The next day, we were ready to search around the outside of the house.

Wild flowers bloomed around the house, along with bushes and crabgrass. We started wide, searching far away from the house. We zeroed in on the house as we searched more and more. We were just a few feet from the house when Tomas called me over to check something out.

Surrounding the house was a brick border, ornate symbols carved into it. On a brick close to the entrance, the carving read "Nothing of occult knowledge or nature, unless invited, may be allowed to enter this area."

"Any deeper meanings with the inscriptions?" I asked Tomas.

Tomas knelt down and felt the grooves of the symbols. "It seems to be designed with the home's owner in mind. Though it's hard to tell with these kinds of symbols. But they're good, real good. This thing could weather hundreds of years without so much as a crack in the barrier. It's almost overkill."

"Overkill?" I asked.

"Yeah, dude, nothing's getting past this thing. At least nothing within the realms of human imagination. Which is crazy because no one's going to bust down the gates of hell just to steal what are essentially bargain-bin cursed items," Tomas explained.

I thought about the strange door in the basement, answering, "Maybe that's not what he's keeping safe."

Tomas got up and brushed himself off. "Then what's our next move?"

As I opened my mouth, I felt the bandages over my chest tighten. A twinge and all of a sudden I felt ill in my stomach. I sat on the grass.

That thing almost killed me. A few more swipes and Matilda would have been waiting for us to return for the rest of time. No one would have known what happened to us. The only reason we got out was because Tomas pulled all the magic he could muster. I on the other hand offered nothing except ideas. I was too weak to beat the creature, the Monitor.

Before this, I was confident I was getting better. I thought I was closer than ever to being the occult investigator Uncle Whitty hoped I could be. Now, it all felt misplaced. Was I not fast enough? Not strong enough?

What level of skill did I need to reach to not be as clueless as everyone else?

Tomas noticed I was staring at space and sat down beside me.

"You doing okay?"

I nodded but didn't answer.

"Hey, you're taking that bruise better than I would have... that can't be the only thing you're beating yourself up about," Tomas said.

I was quiet for a bit, until I said, "I lost to him... I lost to him badly."

"It's nothing that a bit of training can't do," he said.

"Yeah, but what if it isn't just about training? What if my uncle had something about him that I don't?" I said.

"You don't know whether he did or not, so why worry about it?"

"Because he could protect people, and he did it by himself. I can't," I said.

Tomas paused. Shuffling over to face me, he placed one hand on my shoulder.

"You don't know that either," Tomas said. "Maybe we can practice together, so when things get tough, we'll know how to cover for each other. How's that sound to you?"

My face turned red from the setting sun. Revival Fest taught me how to be free without plans, but it felt nice to be given one every so often.

"Tomorrow sounds good," I said.

"Then it's settled." Tomas got up and stretched his arms. "Let's do that after we deal with 'Ms. Grim's demon patch.'"

"Ugh, we already told her the problem was the pH levels," I said, getting up with him.

"That's what I said!" Tomas responded.

With every breakthrough we made to solving our mystery, came more hurdles and issues we needed to solve in the future. The responsibilities of an occult investigator only made that process slower. We couldn't complain, that was the job Tomas and I signed up for.

# CHAPTER 17

In a job like occult investigations, our best practice was out in the field. Which was great since Helford was never keen to be sparse with the strange, no matter how much its citizens wanted the opposite.

We learned quite a few hard lessons since we met that lizard in the mountains. Never trust a mind reader to not cheat at Scrabble, never fight fire spirits with fire demons, and always wear a jumpsuit to missions. The last one was really important, and how we got our official navy blue uniforms. It's the only good thing we got after fighting a sewage monster at Helford's water purifier plant. We called him Crap Shoot.

Even with almost a year's experience under our belts, life still found new ways to keep us on our toes. Today was one of those curveballs.

We'd been running around downtown for the past hour. It was the dead of night, the whole place cleared of people before we started. Not even the bars were open. It was a surreal feeling, a place so full of life now relegated to a testing ground for our new invention. I'd have explored those thoughts more if I wasn't also struggling to stay alive.

A week before we had encountered a monster we called the Invisibeing. I'd describe more about the thing if it wasn't so damn invisible. Nothing could detect it, not even heat sensors. The only reason we knew it was chasing us was that it wasn't very quiet doing so.

It's not easy trying to catch something you can't see. Brilliant minds had done it before, but Tomas and I weren't the best when it came to R&D. The one thing we were able to come up with was the Trap-in-the-box.

The Invisibeing could bench press a car, so the average trap had little effect on it. We turned to magic, turning an innocuous sandalwood box into the occult version of a magical beartrap. Our next issue was drawing the Invisibeing to our trap, and we couldn't think of any better bait than ourselves.

We rounded a corner, sprinting our way into Helford's town square. From previous encounters with the Invisibeing, we knew that it struggled turning. It bought us some time to stop and for Tomas to ready the Trap-in-the-box. Tomas wound the machine crank, placing it down onto the ground.

"With all the stomping that thing's been doing, it might be our biggest catch." I remarked.

"Rather not think of that while prepping a trap we never tested." Tomas said.

I shrugged, "Better now than later."

We both took five big steps away from the box. The alleys echoed the roaring charge of the beast. It sounded distant but got closer with each weighted step.

"Any time now," Tomas said.

"You know you want it," I added.

The steps now reached our street. He marched towards us, his pace matching our heart beats. The reverberations made our eyes rattle in our sockets. Just five more steps, 4 more, 3, 2, and 1.

The trap sprung.

Sometimes I feel like the universe is out to get me. We were so dang close to trapping the Invisibeing. The Trap-in-the-box's strings glowed with magic electric heat. A cloud of purple and blue swirled from the box's entrance.

The creature groaned as it attempted to escape. Though invisible, Tomas and I could tell from the moving strings that it wasn't having a good time. We jumped in the air, dancing under Helford's streetlights. All we needed to do now was call Harriet and take the Invisibeing somewhere where it couldn't cause more damage.

That's when Murphy's law decided to throw its own weight in. One string in the Trap-in-the-box broke, causing the rest to fail. One by one, the glowing orange strings snapped like stretched rubber bands.

I looked at Tomas, and told him to run. It was a good thing we chose to set up the trap in the town, otherwise we'd have nowhere to hide. I ran down one street and Tomas the other. Our plan was to regroup at a rendezvous point. Splitting up made losing the creature all the easier.

I was halfway down Kelly Street, when I heard the Invisibeing stomping close behind. I had two choices, keep running or take a shot at the Invisibeing to buy more time. I chose the latter.

I swung around, aiming my gun at what I assumed was the creature's maw. The moment I did, the creature smacked me with the blind rage only a monster like that has. I got launched through a window and into a tool and paint shop, landing with the grace of a ragdoll. No offense to Matilda. I was lucky enough to have the toolbelt exhibit break my fall instead of the nail exhibit, though the Invisibeing wasted no time throwing that exhibit at me for good measure.

Using my uncle's jacket to absorb the damage, I managed to get out unharmed but was launched further down the shop's paint aisle. Flat on my back, I was exposed to the complex world of paint cans. White, brown, green, and brown but in a lighter shade. That gave me a plan of attack.

I grabbed a paint can and ran to the back of the store. I forgot how heavy full paint cans could be, and the thing caused me to walk with one shoulder higher than the other. I turned to the last aisle on my left: a wall lined with axes, screwdrivers and saws. The important thing to me was they were sharp.

I heard the Invisibeing behind me slink into my aisle. I grabbed a hand ax, running the opposite way it was. Once I had enough distance I knelt down and broke the paint can open. Using my ear alone, I waited until the creature was close enough.

When the time came, I threw the paint into the air. Brown paint fell onto the Invisibeing, covering every welt and wrinkle. The Invisibeing slid in place, confused by the new scent and lack of friction. Taking my chance, I hacked into the creature's front legs.

Translucent blood sprayed about the aisle, making whatever it touched partly invisible. The creature fell onto its back legs, and I took the chance to try to eke out a win. That was a bad idea. I closed the distance, and the Invisibeing punished that move by grabbing me and slamming me against the wall.

Losing the ax, I attempted to wiggle out and escape. The creature pressed me harder into the wall. I felt for another weapon on the wall, grabbing a screwdriver and stabbing its arm until it let me go. It kept up the heat. My vision blurred and my energy drained away. As one act of defiance, I looked straight ahead into whatever eyes it may have had.

It seemed like the end. All my tools were used up, and no one was around to save me. That is, no one I expected to save me.

A shotgun slug ripped into the monster's body. Invisible blood painted the aisle, my ear sent ringing by the explosion. The creature shrieked, its cries answered by another slug destroying what I assumed was its head. The creature slumped down, its legs landing on the checkered tiled floor. I almost slumped to the ground too just before being caught by the man who saved me.

He looked like a gruff Prince Charming. Long black hair and a five o'clock shadow, rocking the look of an action hero.

Holstering his sawed-off shotgun, he asked me, "You alright?"

"Yeah, I actually do this stuff a lot," I stuttered.

"Let's get you out of here."

Soon after, the sheriff and his deputies arrived to dispose of what was left of the monster. Sitting in the back of a patrol car, I collected my thoughts with a cup of coffee. Tomas had just arrived, running over to check on me.

The man who saved me stood in the background. He watched the deputies do their work. When Hush decided to do what Hush does and harass us, the man interjected. Hush looked shocked to see him and was sent back to work without a fuss.

"Is that Chris Evans?" Tomas asked.

I frowned at Tomas. "Did you really just ask me that?"

"I don't know, maybe it was our lucky day," Tomas said.

"Why would that be our lucky day?" I asked.

"Let's change the subject. You okay? Did you get hurt?" Tomas asked.

"No, I'm fine. I just—" I leaned in to whisper to Tomas "I got a bad feeling about this guy."

"How so?" Tomas asked.

"He's just… he's—"

The man approached the car door before I could say anything, asking "You two doing alright?"

"Uh huh," Tomas answered.

The man knelt down to eye level, extending his hand for a handshake. "Name's Charles Nightwood, I'm an occult investigator."

"Oh cool, we're also occult investigators. Name's Tomas."

I shook his hand. "I'm Jonathan Whitlock."

The man stopped at that name, like he was forced into some memory.

"You don't happen to be related to someone by the name Kasper Whitlock?" Nightwood asked.

"That's my Uncle," I said.

"I can't believe it. You're Kasper's nephew. He told me so much about you," he said, a big smile on his face.

That threw me off even more. Ever since I've been in Helford, no one has ever said my Uncle's first name. It's always been "your uncle" and "Mr. Whitlock." This wasn't the distance everyone else gave, it was familiar and heartfelt.

"How did you know my uncle?" I asked him.

"Oh sorry. I should tell you first. I worked with Kasper for a long time. If I hadn't met him, I wouldn't be the person I am now. I was his apprentice, a junior investigator."

I sat there with my mouth open. I had been wondering who my uncle's first apprentice was since Percival first mentioned it. It didn't help that no one in Helford talked about these sorts of things.

"If you're my uncle's apprentice, where have you been this whole time?" I asked.

"Well, I've been traveling the world, going where I'm needed," Nightwood said.

"Ooh sounds like one big road trip," Tomas said.

"A bit more dangerous than the average road trip." Nightwood explained. "But after all that time fighting vampires across state lines, I decided to go see if Helford needed the attention. Though it seems you guys have been handling that stuff."

"Dude you have no idea. We defeated Basket Case, fought a lizard man, and got turnt in Revival Fest, not to mention the wild goose chase we've been having with Percival Maelie." Tomas said.

Nightwood turned his head at that last part. "Percival Maelie? Last I saw that kid, he was still plastering campaign posters for his old man."

"Woah, you really have been gone," Tomas laughed.

I sat there silent as they talked. Too many questions were going in my head. Why did he return to Helford after being gone so long? Why did he even leave in the first place? Through that disarming smile and toned figure was a bunch of secrets I needed to crack open. I was so deep in questions that I didn't notice that I was glaring at Nightwood.

"You okay over there?" Nightwood asked me. "That thing did a number on you."

"Yeah... I'm fine," I said.

"It was nice meeting you two, we should catch up while we have the time," Nightwood said.

"Oh yeah, you know we're just so—"

Tomas interjected, "We can do tomorrow night."

Damn it Tomas, we should have done a huddle for this decision.

"Cool, here's my card if you guys need to talk to me about anything. Stay safe out there," Nightwood said.

He strutted over to his muscle car and drove off into the night. When he was gone, Tomas swung around with stars in his eyes.

"Dude, he's so cool," Tomas exclaimed.

"So cool? He's pretty cool at best," I said.

"What are you talking about? I'd thought you'd be excited about this," Tomas said.

"Look I just… I just have a bad feeling about this guy. All these crazy things with Percival have been unfolding and he decides to show up around when it starts to heat up? That doesn't sit right."

I realized it sounded crazy the moment I said it.

Tomas scooched his way beside me on the patrol car

"I mean, you could see it like that, but you can see it as a chance to find out more about what's been going on. You've said it yourself a million times before, that we need to stop being so in the dark about everything. This might be it."

"It's not just that. I've been thinking. What happens if he decides to stay? What if he decides to take up a job he was trained to do? Maybe I was playing bench warmer this whole time and I just never knew till now," I said, my head lowering more as I spoke.

When I was done, Tomas placed his hand on my shoulder. He looked into my eyes and said, "You ever thought about how much we did this past year? I mean, man, we've done things that would make anyone else roll up into a ball and cry themselves to sleep. That makes you just as much an occult investigator as Mr. Movie Star. No one can say that you don't belong." Looking at the moon, Tomas said "You keep resting here while I get the trap in the box. We'll have a big day tomorrow."

Before leaving, Tomas turned and said "Remember what I said. We're a team so I got your back okay?"

I nodded. "Yeah."

Even after all that Tomas said, doubt still ate at my brain. The world went by slower, and I became unbound by the basic senses that came with like. The more I thought, the more the experience became out of body.

"Belong," I said to myself, my eyes becoming heavy.

# CHAPTER 18

Anyone asking to meet out of town is clearly up to no good.

Tomas and I weren't sure where we were. The instructions Charles had given us had so many left turns that we should have been going in circles. Yet by the end of it, we had ended up an hour away from the farthest edges of Helford.

The spot was a biker bar smack-dab in the mountains. It was straight out of a Western with saloon doors and nails rusting from old wood planks. It even had drunks being thrown out by security, one of them barking, "And stay out!"

The second floor had a row of stolen street signs which read "The Slow Stop."

Entering the bar, things only got weirder. The place was full to the brim with supernatural creatures. A gang of goblin bikers sat at a group of tables. Razor canines gnawed on ribs slathered in barbeque sauce. Green fists knocked at black spiked helmets and leather jacket shoulders.

Other monsters walked solo, resting before going on their own road crusades. We went to the bar to wait for Charles to show up.

I was carrying Matilda, my knee bumping her up and down while we waited. It was hard finding babysitters, including Tomas's mom, who was just as afraid of dolls as her son. We didn't want her to be alone, so we took her along.

Matilda inherited my impatience, so she was soon onto her feet and exploring. Roaming the bar, she bumped into the legs of one of the goblin bikers. He looked down at her, his sharp jaw carving out a look of annoyance. He squatted down to be at her eye level, his lips pursed to show a fence of teeth. His brow narrowed, and Tomas and I readied in case something happened. Matilda, the negotiator she was, raised arms to be held.

Processing this, the goblin laughed. He launched her up onto his shoulders and presented her to the rest of the gang.

"Hey Mozzie, check this kid I found."

Seeing that Matilda was in safe hands, I went back to waiting with Tomas.

To our right, a bat monster hung from the ceiling, using a long straw to drink his cocktail. On our left, a very chatty wild man was talking to the bartender. All except his palms and feet were covered with matted hair. The hair was similar in color to Russian blue cats. The hair on his upper lip was eggshell in color, resembling a moustache. His voice was more human sounding than the other monsters filling the bar.

"You know how all these people are selling coins online or something? What if we made it so that companies paid people in virtual money? They're already using digital cards so why not take the extra step? Wait, why are you walking away? Well more sunflower seeds for me, I guess." Eating from the bowl of sunflower seeds, the wild man's eyes drifted over to us. His eyes widened at the sight of new potential friends.

"Hey guys, how's it hanging? Because I don't know about you, but I'm definitely dangling a bit," he said.

"Yeah, we're alright," I said.

"Air conditioning is a bit to be desired," Tomas added.

"You guys new? I can tell newbies when I see them," the wild man said.

"You mean like new around here, or new to this kind of stuff in general?" Tomas asked.

The wild man gave an unsure shrug. "Whichever you're most comfortable answering."

"We've been doing this for about…" Tomas looked over to me for an answer.

"Half a year," I said.

Tomas nodded like he knew the whole time. "Yep, half a year."

"I'm really happy for you two. Real brave you can be out and proud like that. But don't worry, they may look rough and tumble, but everyone in here is really accepting," the wild man said.

Tomas and I shot a look at each other. "Thank you?"

"So you two are here for a drink, some food, a few rounds of pool?" the Wild Man asked.

"We're here to catch up with someone, his name's Charles Nightwood."

Hearing the name, the wildman almost choked on a sunflower seed.

He leaned over and whispered, "You know Crazy Charlie?"

"You know him?" I asked.

He leaned away, his arm holding onto the bar top to not fall over. "Who doesn't? He's the biggest wild card out there. The creme de la creme of lone wanderers."

"Is that a good or bad thing?" I asked.

"Depends on who you're asking," he laughed.

"What's that supposed to mean?" I asked.

The wild man looked around nervously. When he looked back over to us, he felt around his waist and gave a worried laugh.

"Geez, would you look at that. I seemed to be all out of drinking money. I'll get going so I'm not a burden, it's the nice thing to do."

Before he could get up to leave, I slammed twenty dollars on the bar room table.

I looked to the bartender and then at the wild man.

"Yeah, I'll get something cheap." The bartender slid him a beer. "Name's Branch by the way."

Branch took a sip of his drink, and asked, "So what do you want to know?"

"Let's start with what I already asked," I said.

"Yeah, that. Crazy Charlie's an interesting guy. Either you love him or you hate him," Branch explained.

"Who hates him?" Tomas asked.

"You think I just got a list of that?" He laughed.

"A few examples could help," I said.

Branch began counting with his fingers, answering, "Well you got the Massachusetts Witch Hunters, The Vancouver Vamps, The Order of the Maroon Triangle, Los Angeles Headhunters... Now that I think of it, he's made a lot of enemies that have 'hunter' in their name. Wonder if that's on purpose."

"I doubt that," I said.

"But there's a lot of people who like him too, kinda like Robin Hood but more hot," Branch said.

"Yeah he is." Tomas smiled.

"Don't be ridiculous, he's like a seven at best," I frowned.

"Ooh, that's gotta sting," Branch mumbled.

I glared at him, "What'd you say?"

"Oh nothing, Nothing at all," he blurted.

The more we talked the more confused I got. "If he's such a huge deal, why even come back to Helford?"

"Didn't he tell us he just wanted to come visit?" Tomas asked.

"And we're supposed to trust that? He's literally called Crazy Charlie, he has to be here for something," I said.

"Why can't he just not have an ulterior motive to be here?" Tomas reasoned.

"Because why didn't he get the house then?" I said.

"You know, watching a quarrel in a bar was not a part of my bucket list," Branch added.

"Why are you even a part of this?" I said through my teeth.

Branch looked over at me, his body shrinking at something behind me. "Oh crap, he's here."

"Who?" I turned around.

It was Nightwood standing at the entrance. I heard a crashing sound behind me. Swinging back around, Branch was gone and one of the windows busted through.

"Why does this keep happening to me?" I muttered.

As I was distracted, Nightwood approached us.

"How's everyone doing?" Nightwood said.

"Jesus Christ," I jumped.

"Oh sorry, didn't mean to startle you," Nightwood paused, pointing to the drink Branch left. "Is that yours?"

I grimaced at the drink and responded, "I guess it is now."

Nightwood nodded. "Ah cool, if you want I can get a round after you get finished with that one."

"Oh that won't be necessary," I said.

"Come on guys, I insist. I only get to have a drink with fellow investigators once in a blue moon, so whatever you want, I'll provide it."

Tomas got an IPA, and I decided I would be the designated driver that night. It started out simple, both of us sharing what we'd been up to all this time.

Nightwood seemed pretty impressed with what we managed, especially Basket Case.
"Basket Case, huh? Even Kasper and I had trouble with her," he said.

He was confused about what Percival was up to.

"When I knew him, he was just a kid who took debate class too seriously. I guess I should have seen the signs with how his father was," Nightwood remarked.

Once we were done with our stuff, Nightwood talked about what happened with him. Branch wasn't kidding. Nightwood had made too many enemies to even keep track of. He fought cultists in Louisiana, giants in New York, and ghosts in Las Vegas.

He'd been a drifter, driving city to city with little direction except the goal to help others. He saved lives from monsters and ended curses made by the malevolent. He felt the heat of the Mojave Desert, the humidity of the Florida Wetlands, and the coolness of the Northern Cascades. He made his own journey and he felt complete because of it.

I listened, nodding in false agreement. No way was any of this true. He lived on the road, doing all the things humans need to do in or beside a car. For most people, waking up without a house is one of the worst things someone could go through. He acted like it was the best decision he'd made in his life. He was an inspirational quote wrapped in a free-spirited personality too sweet for taste buds.

I wanted to get up and do something active. My eyes drifted to the dart board, and I had an idea. Pointing to the damaged wall, I challenged Nightwood to a game of darts.

"Sure," Nightwood said as he prepared for his first turn. "Though I do gotta warn ya, I'm pretty rusty."

He proceeded to hit only bullseyes and red spaces on his first turn. The game didn't last long after that. I kept challenging him, trying to find something I could win with. I lost at pool, air hockey, ping pong, even the bar's trivia night. The only game I did win was cornhole, which felt both ironic and disappointing.

At the end of all the games, Nightwood laughed. "Talk about beginner's luck."

"Yeah, you're like an action hero or something," Tomas added.

"He's not an action hero, he's literally just a guy," I said.

"He's right, Tomas, a wise man on a desert plateau once told me that 'humility should be your goal in all things,'" Nightwood said.

This is what nightmares are made of. If it weren't for him having an alibi, I would start to believe Nightwood was sent from hell to kill me. While I was busy rolling my eyes, Nightwood had his eyes on the moving hand of his watch.

His smile disappeared, and when he looked back up to us he said "Hey guys, I know it's a bit sudden, but I think I might have to cut the night short. I got things to attend to right now."

"Aw, man," Tomas exclaimed. He was on his third drink.

Nightwood threw his arms in the air. "I know, I'm feeling the same way."

I was conflicted. He seemed actually bummed out to be leaving, but I couldn't help but feel suspicious. Where did he need to go that was so important? Why was it so close to the town he left behind? Something told me that he was here for more than just reminiscing.

Nightwood waved us goodbye. I sat at the bar, watching through the windows to see which way he turned. He went the opposite way we came from, going further away from town.

Tomas laid his head on the bar, his eyes drooping. I tapped the table, and his body sprung back to life. His eyes looked about in confusion, until landing on me.

"Huh? What is it?" Tomas said.

"Get your head straight, we're leaving."

"Already? We just got here," Tomas groaned.

I narrowed my eyes. "We've been here for two hours,"

"Really? I could have sworn those games went by quicker." Tomas did a short stretch "But seriously, what is it?"

"Nightwood's up to something, and—"

"And your evidence is?" Tomas interrupted.

"You just gotta trust me okay?" I said.

Tomas sighed, closing his eyes. "There's no stopping you, is there? Don't answer that… Just promise me you won't make this a thing."

"Fine, I promise that I'll not stalk every person I find suspicious." I said.

"Bingo," Tomas said. "I'll be needing that in writing when we're done with whatever this is."

Matilda had been giving the goblin bikers emotional advice the whole time we were there.

"Sometimes I feel a bit hurt that we're asked to rough people up all the time," one goblin biker said.

"We could be building people up, but instead we break them down," another said.

I snatched Matilda as she was writing down an answer. I read out her answer before we left the door.

"She says… you guys are independent people who should respect yourselves enough to have 'no' for an answer, and to… get into community work. You gotta build a village to have one to turn to."

They collectively threw their arms in the air, and said, "Why didn't we think of that!

We hurried to our car, swinging out the driveway and into the dark road beyond us.

# CHAPTER 19

Everything was quiet, except the deep hum of moving tires. My eyes tunneled onto the cat's-eyes lighting the middle of the road. We kept our distance, Nightwood's rear lights working as a distant red beacon in the darkness.

The forests went monochrome, trees turning white from high beam lights. Orange eyes of animals peppered the scenery, watching us.

Tomas sat in the passenger seat, eyes closed, holding a water bottle that Matilda gave him. His head pounded from drinking on an empty stomach, and now he was telling me how much he wanted to die.

"Dude, I'm not gonna make it," Tomas groaned.

"Tomas, you've been saying that for the past thirty minutes," I said.

"You got that revolver right?"

"Don't say it," I said.

"Could you do me a favor?" Tomas asked.

"No."

"And just shoot me."

"And there it is, is that water really doing nothing for you?" I said.

Tomas sunk deeper into his head rest. "Nothing that being dead wouldn't fix."

I smirked "And you call me a drama queen,"

"You're a drama queen. I'm a drama king," Tomas said, drifting into sleep.

Ten minutes passed when Nightwood's car made a sudden turn deep into the woods. There wasn't a trail where he was going, so he was off-roading in a muscle car not made to do that. His lights bobbed up and down as he went deeper into the forest. If his car was having trouble, then our car would do even worse.

We parked on the side of the road close to where he turned. Going on foot for the rest of the way, we grabbed whatever monster hunting gear we could. I strapped on a baby carrier, using it to hold Matilda. It wasn't too hard to catch up, though Tomas struggled to follow the pace I was going.

Trailing him got harder the farther we got from the road. It was starting to remind me of our time with the Monitor, except when we did that we were actually prepared to go on a hike. By the time his car had stopped, we were already out of breath. Tomas and I hid behind a thick bush, watching Nightwood from afar.

Nightwood got out of his car, walking to his trunk. Opening it, he pulled an array of equipment including his double barrel shotgun. He gave a quick look around the area and started to trek upwards going up and over a steep hill.

"More hiking? I might for real not make it," Tomas whispered.

We followed Nightwood up the hill and onto flatter terrain. As we did, I checked my phone's map. I hoped that knowing where we were would help us make more sense of the situation. It only made me confused. We were nestled between a mountain range, paralleling a small river leading to a minor lake in the middle of nowhere. The whole place was new territory for me. It screamed suspicious, but not in the way I wanted.

The last month of summer made for a loud forest. Animals used the secure darkness to dart past us. Trees towered over us, shifting leaves making for loud obstacles. The hot air loosened our muscles, both exciting and exhausting us.

We couldn't use our lights to guide us, making Nightwood even harder to keep track of. Thanks to the moon, we weren't completely blind. That is, when there were no clouds in the sky.

I was starting to get used to Nightwood's movements, until he disappeared on us. I don't know how he did it, he passed a tree and was just gone. We were now just wandering, walking beside the river in hopes it would lead to where Nightwood was going.

That all changed when a light flickered in the distance. We stopped, squinting our eyes to see what it was. It got closer, distant voices following suit. Tomas and I hurried to hide, quickly tiptoeing our way behind a fallen tree.

We held our breaths, our backs against the tree. A beam of light went over us, a pair of feet crunching the dry leaves.

"I told you it was nothing," a voice scoffed.

"Look, I could have sworn it was him," another voice said.

"Uh huh, and I'm sure you would have made a big difference against him," the first voice said.

"You're saying it like he's bullet-proof," the second voice said.

"Listen, I've gotten my head knocked around enough to know that being the guy who calls for backup is always better than being the guy who's responding to that call."

"I don't know how you have a job," the second voice responded.

"By being alive, that's how."

Their footsteps got quieter and quieter until we couldn't register them anymore. We crawled away, keeping track of where the light was.

When we found somewhere safe, Tomas whispered, "The heck was that?"

Finally letting myself breathe, I said, "I think whatever Nightwood is after, it's important enough to have armed guards for it."

"This is not the night I wanted to have a stealth mission," Tomas said.

"Just follow my lead, okay?"

We kept going, encountering more guards on the way. They were well armed with military gear and weapons. Yet, they all wore well-tailored suits, with green hoods draped over their heads. They patrolled their areas in small squads, their lights scanning the area for any strange activity.

We shadowed patrols returning back from where they came, breaking away once they rendezvoused with the next shift. Ducking and weaving, we hopped from one patrol to another. The patrols began to make more sense, all of them radiating out from a single point. Checking my map again, the point seemed to be somewhere close to the lake on the side of a hill.

On our second patrol we saw it. It was a fortress masquerading as a log mansion. Stained glass windows decorated the front of the house, its extravagance putting cathedrals to shame. The soft glow of a fireplace emanated from it.

Porches wrapped the entire mansion, spotlights scanning the house's perimeter. Sniper silhouettes dotted the railing, ready to rain hell on anyone stupid enough to approach.

We watched from the bushes. Tomas at this point had been spooked back to consciousness, his eyes wider than they ever were before.

"What reason does Charles have for sneaking around this place?" I asked.

"That should be the least of your worries right now," Tomas said back.

As I planned, Matilda made a light tug at my shoulder.

"Something up?" I asked her.

Matilda pointed at the middle of the driveway. There, a large moving truck was parked. Beside it was a limousine, surrounded by a squad of differently dressed guards. One guard, Tommy gun in hand, opened the back door. Out came none other than the great Percival Maelie.

Seeing him all but confirmed my suspicions about Charles. It can't be a coincidence that the same place Charles was heading was also in the exact spot Percival was. Though that did bring to question that if he was in cahoots with Percival, why was he sneaking around? Either way, he was close by and up to no good. That's what mattered.

Green hooded armed guards ran out from the mansion, standing in a line parallel with each other, forming a pathway from the back of the moving car over to the mansion's entrance way.

With them situated, another man walked out flanked with his own squad of guards. The guards parted, revealing a short man resembling a mobster who fell in a vat of money. He smoked a massive cigar, puffing as he approached Percival. About ten feet from Percival, the man stopped.

The two stared each other down. Taking one hand out his pocket, Percival signaled to the wax guards standing at the back of the moving car. They unlatched and raised the back door.

One by one, in a single file line, living objects hopped down and were escorted away. Naked mannequins, patched up human sized teddy bears, and the ramshackled leftovers of children's dreams. They hobbled past walls of men. Their heads brought low.

"So this what he wanted with the life dust? To make some inanimate slave drive?" I whispered.

Matilda watched the trade, her eyes steady. Her small hand gripped tight on my jacket, shaking.

I patted her head, "We'll get him."

"It looks like they're talking about something down there," Tomas said.

"Damn it, the only way to listen in is to get closer, and we aren't exactly stealthy," I said.

"I am," Matilda wrote on her white board.

Tomas and I traded looks. Matilda could hide in places we never could. We'd have a chance to get vital information on what Percival is doing. The problem was what would happen if she was caught. Either she'd be forced into a life of eternal servitude or shattered on the parking lot pavement.

"You think you can handle it?" I asked Matilda.

"I learned from the best," she wrote with a smiley face.

I smiled while Tomas began to sniffle.

"I swear it's the hangover," Tomas said.

We gave Matilda my phone and a touch pen to type with. The brightness was set to low to not give her position away. Her job would be to get as close as possible and text Tomas what the two men were saying.

She traveled down. Her movements through the bushes were indistinguishable to that of a small animal. She melded into a hedge close to the men, and she began to type.

"Has the product been up to your standards, Mr. Orlando?" Percival asked.

"It has, these unliving servants will work well for tomorrow's banquet," Mr. Orlando responded.

"As I've expected, objects awakened by life dust are highly loyal, easy to train, and lack the need for rest and food that other forms of animation require," Percival said.

"That does bring to question how you got something so rare. Things like that require a great amount of sacrifice," Mr. Orlando said.

"Secrets like that come with high price tags."

"And that price would be?" Orlando asked.

"Nothing you could afford," Percival answered.

Orlando frowned at that answer. He put his cigarette out on the suits of one of the guards and paced around Percival.

"With a favor like this, I'll be expecting a good word from you when I visit the Down Nose Society," Percival said.

"Yes, I'll certainly have words for them, though I doubt they'll be seeing you anytime soon," Orlando said.

"Come again?" Percival said.

"They're rather exclusive. I've served them for years, hosting countless banquets in their honor, and only once have I witnessed one of their official members,"

"Your point being?" Percival queried.

"It'll take more than just gifts to be invited into their ranks," Orlando said.

Percival was quiet for a second, then said, "Their leader's a rather interesting man… so powerful that even death can't touch him."

Mr. Orlando scoffed. "You say that like you met him."

I texted Matilda, "Time to get going, we got what information we needed."

Matilda attempted to leave quietly, but her movement caused the hedge to shift. In a split second, every single guard aimed at the bush. They were about to shred the bush when Percival raised his hand to stop them.

He approached the brush, crouched down, and peered into it.

"He's looking at me," Matilda texted. "He smiled."

Percival took his head out.

"It was just another animal, no need to worry," Percival said.

The deal then went as it did before. All the life dust servants led into the cabin, and Percival left with his wax mobster goons. Things settled back to their status quo.

Matilda escaped back to us. Tomas and I hugged tight onto her. We were given some context on the place, but one question was still in the air.

"How are we supposed to get past that?" I said to myself.

Tomas nodded. He pointed to the left side of the mansion. "What about that?"

I squinted. "Looks to be a garage."

"Think there's enough bushes for us to hide?" Tomas asked.

"Not enough for us to not get noticed by snipers."

"Then I got an idea," Tomas said

We swung around to the garage side of the house. Getting in position, Tomas got his magic gloves on. Lifting his arm, he concentrated. Thin red strands flickered over the tips of his fingers. As they did, the spotlights began to flicker as well.

Confused, the snipers searched for any threats in the darkness. Going at a heartbeat rhythm, the spotlights brightened more and more. Hitting a fever pitch, the front spotlights erupted in a mass array of sparks.

The guards who hadn't been dazed ran to the front entrance, expecting the disturbance to be there. Snipers left their original post, hoping to offer support against what they thought was one man.

We burst from the bushes, dashing across the driveway into the garage. Hiding beside a million dollar car, Tomas and I caught our breath. The garage's interior was long, able to store a host of different cars. If the outside wasn't evidence enough, whoever owned these cars was very wealthy.

We crawled to the door leading further in, the sound of commotion happening behind us. Through the door was a spacious kitchen, its granite island the size of a studio apartment. The sound of heavy footsteps went over us, traveling down a set of stairs to where we were. Three guards entered the kitchen, going to the side opposite from us.

We pressed against the island to hide. I pushed against the floor. My foot slipped, screeching against the marble surface. The guards went silent, the sounds of their footsteps getting closer. I gripped my revolver. My gun wouldn't kill them, but it could stun them long enough to get the drop on them. I didn't want to kill anyone, but at that point, I doubt I would live to regret it.

I made my peace, readying to leap up and fire. Just before I did anything stupid, Charles Nightwood burst into the scene. Diving through the nearest window, he knocked out the guards with a mix of punches and grapples. Tossed over the kitchen island, the last guard crashed into the pantries directly in front of us. Charles was gone by the time we poked our heads up.

"Dude, that was insane," Tomas whispered loudly in my ear.

I breathed harder than I ever had before. Reality clocked in, and a part of me wanted to run for the hills. Yet that part of me also said I couldn't without Tomas wanting to too.

"You wanna just call it quits?" I said.

Tomas looked at me like I lost it. "You should have said that hours ago!"

"I—I don't know. I didn't know what I signed us up for, okay?" I said.

"Yuh huh, and we didn't do that with any of the other stupid things we did either," Tomas collected himself. "Look, Jonathan, you never stopped being one hundred percent before. What makes this any different?"

It really wasn't different to anything we did before. We'd gotten out worse, the only difference was I had someone to compare myself to. Nightwood was my uncle's first choice, not some last minute surrogate like I was. He was smarter, stronger, and more talented. If he had stayed as Helford's friendly neighborhood occult investigator, Percival Maelie may have not been an issue from the very beginning. The problem wasn't ever about not trusting him. It was about me, and what I thought I wasn't.

Tomas looked at me, eyes wide waiting for an answer.

"I am having the worst hangover right now. I'd fight god to make it stop, and trust me, you'd do that on a normal day. You're literally the most insane person I've met. You don't have the right to get cold feet now."

Realization coursed through my head and down to my toes and fingertips.

My uncle's note echoed in my mind. "The rest of the family isn't made for it, but you are."

Maybe that's what my uncle meant. I'd been fighting tooth and nail just to find out if I could. I survived the trials. Why doubt myself now?

Feet rustled on the floors above us, commotion building throughout the home.

"Seems like we're needed," I said.

"That's my Jonathan!"

We ran up the stairs, our weapons of choices at arm's reach. The halls were straight out of an Agatha Christie novel. Flower-shaped lights gave the varnished walls a copper shine. Red carpets built a road lined with gold. The hall flickered, Tomas's magic continuing to affect the house's electricity.

In that flickering, someone appeared. He was enveloped in black clothing resembling a straitjacket. Heavy straps covered his body, giving the illusion of restraints. His legs twisted around each other in a ballerina's pose. His face was a muted white, contrasting the wild black which covered him from head to toe.

Tomas and I froze, unsure of what he was. We'd fought a lot of things, but he was something new. What I was sure about was he was nothing like the guards we encountered before.

He lowered his hands, revealing that each of his fingers had been replaced by garden shears. They were polished, the only well-kept thing about him.

Eyes wide, the stranger cocked his head. "Well, you're not Charles."

# CHAPTER 20

It was a hallway standoff. The stranger was as still as water. We were still too, though we wore it worse than he did. What sounded like a war raged outside, adding to the tension in the air.

"Can't we go a day without fighting some freak of the week?" Tomas exclaimed.

"Hey, we can't just skip to 'name calling' already. We just met him," I said.

"Your friend is right, I am not something to be reasoned with," the stranger said.

I sighed, muttering, "The one time I try to be nice." I then spoke up, saying "So what's your deal? I'd say evil gardener, but you don't got the tan for it."

The stranger took a step forward. "What would be the point when I'd just be flaying you anyways?"

His voice was flat, sharp and to the point.

"Considering how you called Charles by his first name, you wanted something personal. It'd be a real downgrade to kill two people who know nothing about you," I said.

The stranger stopped and tapped his chin with one of his fingers.

"I guess it would be an interesting change of pace," he said, shrugging.

Tomas leaned into my ear, and whispered, "How the heck do you always get these nutjobs monologuing for you?"

"I wish I knew," I said.

"My name is Todd Shearfingers, Shear Todd for short. I am a man-made automaton. My gears are muscles and my iron is blood. I've served my master for many years, and in that time I've gained a new plaything, Charles

Nightwood. Once I'm done with you, I'll see what my new upgrades can do to him."

"I don't think that last part came out right."

"Tomas!" I leered.

"What?" Tomas said.

"But now I'm curious, who are you two?" Shear Todd said.

"I'm Jonathan Whitlock and he's Tomas," I said.

"Whitlock? Seems familiar." Shear pondered, a soft smile forming.

"Trust me, you'll be remembering us real soon," I said, pulling my pistol.

"Oh ho! Don't threaten me with a good time."

Shear rushed towards us, his blades flared out in murderous glee. I fired three shots, aiming two for the chest and one for the head. Shear shielded his face with a bouquet of metal fingers. The shot aimed for the head ricocheted, bullet fragments sparking off like fireworks.

The two body shots went through him, black gore coating the walls. He raced towards us on all fours, his bloodlust more than rivaling anything we'd fought before.

Tomas went in, concentrating a massive amount of magic into the carpet in front of us. The rug set fire, and Tomas sent the flame toward Shear in a rippling wave. Shear stuck onto the walls like a cat from hell, avoiding whatever inferno we sent him. Not wanting to become his new scratching post, I grabbed Tomas and ran into the room beside us.

Slowing down isn't easy with blades for fingers. Shear struggled with the physics involved, giving us extra time while he was stuck slowing down in the hallway.

The room we were in was a small empty bedroom.

"He's been defending his head, it might be a weak point," I said to Tomas.

Tomas rolled up his sleeves. "Let's see what he can do with the whole place falling on him."

"How long will that take?" I asked.

"With a house in this kind of condition? More than a minute," Tomas said.

"Oh crap," I muttered.

Shear appeared at the door, an uncontrollable smile twisting over him. He swung his face between Tomas and me, his mind confused with the devilish decision of who to kill first. I put a stop to his sadistic trolley problem by aiming my gun at him.

He lurched towards me, attempting to slap my gun out of my hands. I took two steps back, avoiding his first few swings. Catching up to me, Shear brought his claws into a downwards sweep.

With the attack aimed to hit Matilda, I threw my arm up to guard her. Sharpened blades sliced off strands of hair, one of them cutting into my cheek. They were stopped only by the magical toughness of my uncle's jacket.

"Jonathan," Tomas cried out.

"Ignore me… god damn it," I strained.

Muscles tensed and shook, my arm struggling to hold up against the strength of monsters beyond human. Blood dripped off my chin and onto Matilda's curled black hair. With my other hand, I swiped Shear away with my newly acquired hand axe. The same one I used to fight the Invisibeing.

Shear leapt away, creating distance between us. His body heaved in what approximated a laugh.

"Now that was fun. You make for someone really comfortable to fight with, just good enough to be a challenge, but not so great as to be a threat," Shear said.

I was breathing heavy enough to provide oxygen for ten men. There was a distinct taste of metal in the back of my throat. It had the tang of loss.

This was my second go against a monster both quick and nimble. He might have been two leagues below the last one, but all that meant was that we were at a similar level of skill. I was on my own, same as before.

I scoured the memory cabinets. There had to be some strange plan or esoteric solution that I hadn't noticed before. It couldn't be easy, it had to be complicated.

Then I remembered Revival Fest. The serene existence that ran through my fingertips. The heartbeat thumping in my ear. Tomas described it as cause and effect, the unseen plans our world makes every single day. Our perceptions make it seem unpredictable, yet the method nonetheless persists. At that moment, I had everything I needed.

"That's an interesting look. Are you realizing I'm not some plaything?" Shear said.

"Forgive me, because I should really be thanking you right now," I beamed, wiping the blood from my face.

Shear raised an eyebrow. "And I'm the crazy one here."

"Don't worry, I'm real lucid right now. Better savor that free hit you got on me, it's going to be your last."

He ran at me with another mad flurry of attacks. I kept my distance, knocking each attack away with my ax. He struggled more, becoming frustrated with each missed swing. He got closer, and I followed suit. We whirled around the room, jacket and axe countering a clamping steel maw. Shear's smile disappeared, his face warped by the sour taste that results from real effort.

"I don't understand, what changed?" Shear spat "Why are you so hard to beat?"

I held his arms away, his blades only an inch away from my face, "I'd might as well toy with how seriously you've taken this."

I knocked him away, and again he came back for more.

My hunch was being proven right in real time. Even with the speed Shear had over me, he had one thing that slowed him down more than anything else. He was a machine. Flesh and blood, yet still mechanical at heart. His swings were predictable, following the logic of gears and springs. He could move, but only at the range of a pendulum.

When it was time for him to crank up an attack, I would move to be an inch out of range. If he tried to switch up tactics, I would move in closer to force him into the same decisions that made him so easy to avoid. The world was running circles around him, and I was moving with it.

Shear, frustrated, did a desperate lunge. I made a simple side step, maneuvering behind him. Pulling my pistol, I fired three shots into him. He stumbled forward, ending up in the center of the room where we needed him.

"Tomas, sink him!"

Tomas then did what he did best. The ceiling above Shear bowed downwards. Red strands flickered, magic appearing like visible radiation. The boil then exploded out, collapsing onto Shear. The force of the magic attack went even further, causing the center to give out and fall down to the first floor.

Tomas and I hugged the walls of the room, where the floor held up. We both peeked over. The room below us was a massive living room, complete with a bar, pool table, trophy display and book cases.

"Dang, man, you have outdone yourself," I said to Tomas.

"I work to impress," Tomas said with a prideful smile.

Assessing the pit, I said, "I really doubt Charles is down there."

"Yeah, but we also can't leave Baby Scissors down there as an unchecked threat either," Tomas added.

I took Matilda out of her carrier and placed her on the ground.

Kneeling down, hand on her shoulder, I asked "You think you got it in you to do one more thing for me?"

Matilda nodded.

"I need you to go out and find Charles. You'll probably blend in with all the other dolls, so you don't need to worry about being spotted, just be safe and out of the way, okay?"

Matilda considered for a bit, then wrote, "I won't let you down."

"I knew you wouldn't," I said.

Matilda shimmied over to the door and skipped out of view. Tomas looked like he was watching his daughter grow up and go to college.

"I thought you hated dolls?" I smiled.

"I guess she grows on you," he said, and shrugged.

Sliding down a dresser into the living room, Tomas and I assessed the debris. Chaos echoed through the mansion, the sounds of Charles doing his thing.

Going to the bar, Tomas asked, "This has been fun and all, but why are we even here? Scratch that, why is Charles here?"

"Maybe there's a magical item of some sort. Whoever owns the place has the money for it," I said, walking to the trophy display.

The display had the usual things people expect. Football trophies lined the shelves, along with decorated whiskey glasses and souvenirs. What drew my eye was the center shelf. On it was a sword. It was single bladed and felt strangely medieval amongst everything else. I picked it off its display and examined it.

As I did, something exploded behind me. A bloodcurdling screech came after along with clanging of metal.

Tomas hollered "Look out!"

I didn't waste a second. I swung around, pulling the blade in an upwards arc. The sword carved into Shear's extended arm. Shear's eyes widened, a look of both fear and surprise. His arm flew off, clattering down like a drawer of silverware. Oil colored blood poured out, turning the floor into a deep pit of darkness.

Everyone stood in silence, shocked by what just happened. Shear looked down, dejected. I brandished the blade, somewhat confused at how I did that. I did a lot of things, but none of them were that cool.

I didn't know how to follow up after that, so I just said, "Are you done yet?"

Shear stepped away, tripping over the rubble. I was about to go to Tomas when two more freaks decided to show up.

The double doors leading out of the room burst off their hinges. From that insane entrance came a troll and a human-sized pixie buzzing behind him.

"Great, more things to fight, you're looking less talkative than bush barber over there," I said.

"Yep," The troll nodded.

The pixie wasted no time firing a barrage of magic missiles while the troll ran in to attack. I raced to Tomas, jumping behind the bar with him.

"Now's the time to use big magic, Tomas," I said.

"I can't, I need to recharge to do something like that," Tomas explained.

A corner of the bar exploding beside us.

"Where the hell are people hiring monsters as bodyguards?" I asked.

"You think I know?" Tomas said.

"You're the smartest between us, so I had hope," I answered.

"Aw, thank you."

Three bottles of whiskey shattered over us.

"On my mark, you distract while I shoot," I said.

I reloaded while Tomas grabbed a liquor bottle.

"Now!"

We sprung up. I fired a volley at the Troll while Tomas threw the bottle at the face of the pixie. Our marks were made, but they weren't enough to down the monsters.

Taking offense to his newfound bullet wounds, the Troll lifted one of the couches to throw at us. That was until his chest got blown open with a shotgun slug. The Troll fell to the ground dead with the couch resting atop his body. It was Charles Nightwood, having entered the room by swinging down from one of the windows.

The Pixie tried in vain to fight back but did as well against a shotgun as the troll. Seeing an opening, Shear hurtled himself to spear Charles as he reloaded. He would've killed Charles if it weren't for a bullet going straight through one of his temples and out the other. Shear crumpled to the ground, my revolver smoking at the hip.

Finally recognizing us, Charles said "Johnathan? Tomas? What are you doing here?"

I started to laugh nervously. "Well that's a long story because—"

"He was jealous," Tomas interrupted.

"Tomas," I exclaimed.

"What? I'm just being honest," Tomas said back.

"Thank all that's mighty that your porcelain friend told me in time, you would have been mincemeat by those automatons otherwise," Charles said.

"I thought Shear was the only automaton here," I said.

"All of the monsters under Mr. Orlando are automatons. He pays good money to have guards that won't betray him," Orlando explained.

Looking down, both the fae and troll bled the same black blood as Shear. Creeping up to my shoes, the ichor gave my feet a tingling sensation like my foot had fallen asleep.

Taking my mind off the bodies, I asked "Where's Matilda?"

"I don't know, she went the opposite way you guys were, said she had things she needed to deal with personally," Charles answered.

Tomas and I traded looks.

"Either way, what are you doing here, and how can we help?" I asked

Charles sighed, making peace with the fact we were there now. "I'm looking for an ornate wood cylinder. Something important is inside it. I haven't been able to find it."

"We are in the trophy room, so maybe it's somewhere around here?" Tomas said.

The three of us looked over the cabinets. None of them matched the description. Taking a second look at the bar, something familiar came into view. Behind the bar and under the counter was a symbol. The same one Tomas and I saw at the burnt down home of the secret society. Percival

had mentioned their name.

"Is this related to the Down Nose Society?"

Charles froze. His silence was proof enough.

Feeling under the bar for anything, my hand

brushed over something.

It was a knob, similar to ones used for drawers.

Except, it wasn't connected to one. I pulled at the knob,

which made a distinct click. A circular piece of the bar rose

up. Pulling that piece out revealed the wood cylinder.

Around the piece was an engraved artwork. It showed

hooded figures surrounding a massive hand in the sky. At

the end of each finger was a string which reached to the

bottom. I showed Charles. He thanked me, placing it in his

duffle bag.

"We gotta get out of here quick," Charles said

"Before—"

An ocean of green-hooded guards poured in. They surrounded us, weapons at the ready in case we tried anything. The three of us showed our hands where they could see them.

"Alright, no need to get hasty here, we surrendered," Charles said.

The guards parted, revealing Mr. Orlando.

"Charles Nightwood, I was praying I wouldn't have to see you again," Mr. Orlando said.

"I can say the same thing for you, Mr. Orlando," Charles said.

"I can't stop what I am, Mr. Nightwood." Noticing Tomas and I, Mr. Orlando then asked, "Who are these two?"

"They're my colleagues, and that's all you need to know," Charles responded.

"I can't say that's very hospitable, you being in my house and all," Orlando said.

"You two required to have this little back and forth every time you meet?" I said to Charles and Orlando.

"You're one to talk," Tomas said.

I leered at Tomas.

"Mr. Nightwood has made it his mission to make my life miserable, every time he appears, he finds a new way to destroy or steal my property," Orlando said.

"Like I'd let you sit comfortably while you leech off the work of entire communities," Charles said back.

"You can have that opinion, Nightwood, but it won't save you," Orlando said.

Orlando kept monologuing. A few of the guards even started scrolling their phones. Standing there, arms toward the sky, made me realize how tired I was. I wasn't prepared for this, and I had run out of my normal tricks. Besides, there was nothing in my toolkit that could help me fight off an army of armed guards. I'd have been more worried if I wasn't so exhausted.

As my eyes started drooping, Tomas leaned close to my ear and whispered, "I'm finally able to do that big magic you wanted."

My eyes widened. "I'm not stopping you."

"Be ready for the big click," Tomas said.

"The what?" I said.

Then Orlando finished his speech. "And now you will die. Fire!"

The guards aimed their weapons and pulled their triggers. Their guns clicked, nothing. All of the guards looked at each other, confused. Squinting, I noticed the faint red strands collecting around their rifles.

"Charles, now!" I shouted.

We pulled our weapons but were still outnumbered. Guards readied themselves with brass knuckles and batons. Even without guns, they'd still overwhelmed us.

Guards piled towards us. One guard leading the charge pulled his fist back to strike me. Before he could, a massive teddy bear barreled down from the floor above us and flattened him. Dust shot up, the green hooded guards fixed in place by the presence of the bear.

The teddy bear stood upright, weighted beads shifting inside its rotund body. Blue button eyes watched with blank judgement. Resting on one of the bear's shoulders was our porcelain daughter.

"Matilda?" Tomas and I said.

Turning to face us, Matilda presented her white board. Written in red marker were the words "Revolt!"

More living objects fell down to join us. Cloth puppets stepped down on long stilts. Long sock monkeys helped down mannequins, dolls, crash test dummies, and much more. We had the whole toy box standing at our side.

"You heard the girl! Attack!" I yelled.

We charged the guards in front of us. These guys were well trained, but not for this. Guards broke away, not wanting to get trampled by the therapy bear.

"What are you doing? Run at them!" Orlando said.

"Seems you ran out of people willing to do suicide charges for you," I said.

"Mark my words, Charles, I will find your friends, and when I do they will suffer," Orlando said.

"Yeah we're not starting this, let's leave," I said.

The four of us, along with our animated army, ran out of the house and into the forest. Walking out, I noticed all the destruction Tomas and I didn't cause. Knocked out guards littered the halls, and bullet holes riddled the house's wood pillars. I still couldn't wrap my head around the fact it all came from one guy. Charles was something else.

Leaving through the forest was a lot easier than entering through it. The guards who were on patrol ran the opposite direction we were going. With all the magic interference going on, they had no idea whether we were still at the house or not. They made the best choice they could, which just so happened to be the wrong one.

Gravity helped us as we ran downhill to where our cars were. Closer down, the army of living stuffies broke off from where we were going. The bear handed me Matilda.

"Are you sure about going? I could find a place where you guys could live safely in Helford," I said.

"There's always room for crazy stuff where we live," Tomas added

Matilda helped translate for the other living objects, writing "We want to, but doing so could endanger your home, and you've already done so much for us."

"If that's your choice, I won't stop you, just know that we're close by if you need somewhere to turn to," I said.

"Thank you for your kindness," the bear bowed.

He then turned to Matilda, "And thank you for reminding us that we could be free."

The living objects disappeared into the darkness. Wherever they went, it was by choice and not by force.

Getting to his car, Charles hid his bag and gave us a piece of paper with coordinates written on them.

"Make sure you're not followed. I'll be waiting."

Charles then dropped us off at our car, and sped away when we got out of the forest. We drove like the world was about to end. I didn't want to look back, everything already felt too dangerous for my own good.

After a bit of driving, Tomas said, "How do we always keep pissing people off?"

That made me pause. "I don't know,"

Tomas dozed off as he spoke. "At least I got you to deal with it,"

Good thing it was so dark, I had a hard time not smiling.

# CHAPTER 21

We hid in a motel at the edge of town. Tomas was in the room, his hangover dragging him into deep sleep. Charles packed away his monster-fighting equipment.

I sat guard outside in my lawn chair. It was still dark, stars twinkling through shrouds of clouds. Bugs chattered in the distance, only silenced by the rare car driving by.

My nerves had cooled since, and I took my time outside to breathe the fresh air. A lot has changed about me since I moved to Helford. I didn't have a plan before. I technically didn't have one now, but now I had some direction.

Before I went to Helford, my biggest goal was just to have something to do. Now I was fighting the supernatural, and I couldn't be happier. I should have been scared of that thought, younger me would have been. Yet, I wasn't afraid at all. A purpose in life can make you do stupid things.

As I contemplated my life choice, Charles came outside and sat beside me. He handed me a cold bottle of water. As I drank, he examined the wood cylinder we worked so hard to get.

"You know what it does?" I asked.

"If I'm being honest, no. Something's rattling inside, that's the best I can tell you," Charles said.

"What was the point of stealing it then?" I asked further.

"I was in Atlanta thwarting the plans of a supernatural being by the name of Jones Hook. He has a lot of influence in the supernatural underworld, meaning he had no shortage of people who wanted him off the map. One of those people was someone in his inner circle. They had some interesting dirt on him, said Jones Hook was involved in a secret society, one that everyone else I talked to said was long dead. She also told me that an important piece in finding this society was in one of these," Charles said, brandishing the cylinder up like a baton.

"Then why go here? Seems like stealing from Jones Hook would have been closer," I said.

"You kidding me? I can give his operations a few light bruises, but stealing from the man himself was something else entirely. I had to look somewhere else, which led me to find out that Orlando had been buying an odd amount of old antiques from a little town called Helford."

"So that's it? You just came here by mere coincidence?" I said.

Charles sighed. "I'd be lying if I said I came just for that."

"Then why did you?" I asked.

Charles looked on at the silent road, the cicadas' words filling the empty space.

"The nights always sounded so busy around here. It's like this place just refuses to be in the middle of nowhere. These were the prime times when Kasper and I would go out and solve whatever mysteries Helford had to offer. It's weird knowing he's not out there anymore."

I pressed into my seat. For most of my life, my family told me that my uncle was a hermit. He'd been made to seem isolated, one dot in a vast painting. That idea had stuck with me more than I realized. It was hard to imagine those experiences with my uncle as anything but unique. I believed I was the only bit of human connection he had. It was clear now that none of that was true. Maybe that's why I was mad at Charles, for breaking down a clear lie. One that if destroyed would prove I knew as much about my uncle as everyone else. I should have felt sad about it. Instead I was coasting on a new angle in reality.

"Everything okay?" he asked.

"Yeah, though in a weird way," I said.

"Why is that?"

I took a sip of my water. "Things feel too good, you know? Like if anyone else was going through the things I've gone through, they'd have lost their minds. I feel like I shouldn't be feeling alright about it."

Charles smiled, nodding in understanding. "I said that very thing to Kasper."

"You did?" I asked.

"Yep." He nodded. "It was maybe a year into my training. We'd been fighting a monster that ate people's dreams. It was stronger than either of us had expected. It managed to elude us for almost a month before we caught it off guard. Our big plan was to destroy it on its home turf. Kasper had trained so that once the monster entered his mind he could pop the monster with a single thought. But the monster saw through our plan, and instead of going for him, it went for me."

"Jeez, how did you get out of that?" I asked.

"I did what Kasper was going to do. I never practiced it a day in my life, but I knew the basics of it. It almost killed me, but I managed to do the impossible and destroyed it," Charles said.

"Doesn't sound too fun," I said.

"That's what I thought too. Then an hour passed, and I was the happiest I'd ever been then," he said.

"But why?" I stammered. "Am I just crazy? It doesn't really make sense."

"We're all a bit crazy." Charles paused to think, reclining in his chair. "Remember what you told me about Revival Fest? How you felt meeting them?"

"Yeah?" I said.

"After everything you did, after all that partying and fighting, you felt at peace. The reason why isn't because of the fighting or even partying. The reason why is that you conquered your fears about living on the edge and became a new person because of it. You lightened the load essentially."

I sat there speechless. The only word I could find in the end was "Huh."

Charles seemed to understand, and added, "We grow a lot more than we realize, that's a part of being human. The most important part being how we grow."

Pulling up the will to ask, I said, "Why did you part ways with my uncle?"

Charles's smile lessened. "I wasn't good at school, and my family didn't have the money to make up for it. Kasper came around that time when I needed someone to tell me I was something. But after a while, reality started to weigh in and I got scared about my future. Everyone around me was becoming doctors, teachers, and accountants while I was still hunting monsters in the forest. I needed some soul searching, so I left."

I reclined in my chair and looked back at my own life.

"You think that'll happen to me? That I'll end up feeling trapped in this job?" I asked.

Charles's smile returned. "Of course not."

"But everything I'm doing is so similar to what you did," I said.

"Because you have everything I didn't. You have the trust of the whole town and friends who believe in you. I would have never left if I had what you have now."

"Oh," I said.

Charles continued. "Besides, you can't leave now without Tomas. He is in love with you."

"Wait, what?" I blurted.

"What, you didn't notice?"

My face started heating up "I mean… I guess I didn't recognize the signs."

Charles laughed, giving a light tap on my shoulder "Didn't recognize the signs? You met him in his backyard and now he fights monsters with you. What more hints do you need?"

I felt the back of my neck, which was now hotter than a stove turned high.

"I mean yeah… but… uh… you really think so?" I said.

"The first thing I learned on the road was how to look out for signs," Charles said.

I smiled, letting silence take over for a bit. The sky turned a lighter shade of blue. The sun began to make its presence known.

Maybe Charles was right. I was changing. I just hoped that it was for the good of everyone else, Tomas especially.

# CHAPTER 22

It was eight in the morning, Tomas was cooking up breakfast, and I was finding a show for Matilda to watch. Things had been slow in a way we weren't quite used to. Even Ms. Grim's garden, which did turn out to have actual little demons in it, was resolved without much issue.

My original theory was that the lull was from Charles. He was still kicking around Helford, perhaps doubling as a deterrent for those more reasonable monsters. Though that idea held less water as Charles did his own set of investigations outside the public eye.

We had more room in the day to rest. We started waking up earlier, a foreign concept to us after almost a year of late night monster hunting. Tomas went deeper into studying magical concepts, while I used my time to fix

Uncle Whitty's aging telescope. We often did both activities together, enjoying each other's presence in the working silence.

Today seemed to be going through the same sort of motions. We talked through the dividing space the hallway made through the kitchen and living room. I was searching up Matilda's favorite movie, "Toy Story." She related with the characters, and she also became obsessed with pretending to be a toy when people were visiting. Our poor customers didn't suspect a thing before she leapt at them. Tomas made his family's famous pancakes. It was their best kept secret, meaning Tomas took a picture of the recipe the moment his mom wasn't looking.

"You said he was going where tomorrow?" Tomas asked, mixing spices into the batter.

"Somewhere in Florida called Citrus Valley. His informant's meeting him down there," I answered.

"So where is he right now?" Tomas asked.

"He said he was looking into some offhanded thing my uncle said once."

"I'm good as long as we don't climb more mountains," Tomas said.

Seeing my chance, I said, "I'd climb your mountain."

"Huh?"

"Hm?"

"I didn't hear you, what did you say?" Tomas yelled.

"Oh nothing," I yelled back.

Matilda's eyes gave a knowing glint. She looked at the TV, then at me.

"We'll marathon the whole series if you forget all about this," I said to her.

"Deal," Matilda wrote back.

At a quarter to eight, we got a letter in the mail. Small, pink and covered in glitter, I brought it in at an arm's length. We hovered over it, wondering who it could be from. Living in the middle of nowhere made letters a special event for us. We even tallied every time we got junk mail.

"Any idea who it could be?" Tomas asked me as he laid pancakes out on the dinner table.

"Not really, you?" I said.

"I don't know anybody who would send that much glitter," Tomas smirked.

I opened the letter, picking at the glitter sealed around the folds.

Tomas pulled the pancakes back to avoid the splash zone. "Dude be careful, these pancakes are premium."

I released the letter from its fancy prison, brandishing it for a bit before opening.
In fine cursive, the letter read:

"Dear friends, I have a grand offer for you. Go to city hall. I'll explain more in due time."

I read it aloud, Tomas looking more confused as I read.

"That's it?" Tomas said.

I shrugged.

"I don't know. No one goes through all this effort just to ask for a meeting somewhere else. Sounds like a trap," Tomas said.

I collected the glitter into the trash, and said, "Maybe Percival's behind this. The guy's obsessed with making deals. Doesn't explain all the glitter though."

"That only adds to how sketchy this is," Tomas said.

I looked over the letter, thinking of all the possible people who might have sent it. "But why city hall?"

"Nostalgia? He used to be mayor," Tomas said.

I got up from my chair, grabbing my uncle's coat. Tomas followed me around the house, confused.

We grabbed our stuff from room to room, Tomas saying to me, "Why? We know it's a trap, we're losing nothing by ignoring it."

"We would be losing something by not going," I said, handing Tomas his magic gloves. "We have a chance to catch him off guard. Besides, Percival is dangerous, and it'd be irresponsible to just leave him out in the open like that."

Tomas shot an intense look. You'd have thought us fighting everything under the sun would make us more careful of the dangers. Instead it made us more aware of what we'd risk by taking our time. Maelie hadn't been volatile before, but dangerous things always seemed to follow when he was around.

Tomas made a deep sigh. "I hate that you're right, you know that?"

We showed up expecting Percival, but what we got was something else entirely.

Glitter tendrils twisted towards the sky, working up in a column of pink. Magic aura emanated from it like the heat from a fire, burning city hall in an inferno of glamour.

The people inside lay dormant, reaping the sleeping beauty's curse. Interns made keyboards into pillows, jumbled letters filling computer screens. Bookkeepers relaxed over files scattered on cold tile floors. Light breathing expelled lungs full of sparkling dust. In her office Mayor Maelie slept, face flat on the cold slab desk.

The shocking part was the building was already like that when we got there. We managed our way in, and when we got out the police were there waiting for us.

Tomas and I stood with our arms raised high in the air. The dark clouds above stirred with the emerging arcane smoke. Sheriff Hush and his deputies had us surrounded, jumping from their patrol cars with guns armed and sirens blaring.

"Jonathan Whitlock and Tomas Seer, you are under arrest!" Sheriff Hush said through his speaker.

"We don't sleep in one time, and this happens!" Tomas said.

At that moment, I couldn't agree with him more.

"Sheriff Hush, you need to listen to us, we didn't do it," Tomas said.

"Yeah, if we waste any more time, whoever did this might have already covered their tracks." I said.

"Shut your traps, you two! You've been causing trouble since you got here. I knew it was only a matter of time before the freak and loner went over the edge. Deputies, arrest them!"

I looked at Tomas. "You know what to do."

Tomas threw his arms, sending a wave of magical interference. The deputies' guns became Murphy's law's playground. Rounds fed wrong, firing pins broke and safeties were suddenly switched on.

The deputies fumbled with their guns, and we took our chance. We ran, the deputies struggling to catch up. We'd gotten enough practice running. A year of fleeing from monsters does that. Diving into our car, we sputtered it to life and drove off.

Behind the wheel, Tomas said "Where the hell are we going?"

"I don't know," I said.

"You better think of something because home is not an option," Tomas said.

Even though our home had a spell protecting the house, it was designed against people and things involved in the supernatural. The spell would do nothing against the Sheriff and his deputies, and neither of us were interested in a police siege.

"We got those suits in the back trunk," I said.

Police sirens began to blare behind us.

"We'd need to lose them first to do that," Tomas said.

I thought quickly, and then I remembered. Crawling into the back seats of the car, I dug around the floors.

"It's gotta be somewhere around… there!" I got up from the floor, my knife boomerang in hand.

"Oh my god, I thought you lost that at Revival Fest."

"I bagged Percival's, no way I'm losing out on something I paid sixty bucks for," I said.

I pushed myself halfway through the window, facing the patrol cars behind us. I aimed for the tires, using the point of the knife boomerang as an iron sights. My eyes were close to shut to protect from the stray water droplets coming down. I pulled my arm back and threw it. The boomerang twisted in the air, buzzing past tires as a saw blade of destruction.

The leading patrol car's right tires exploded, causing it to slide sideways. Attempting to swerve out of the way, the cars behind lost cohesion and created a domino effect of car crashes. Having done its job, the boomerang flew off to the great beyond where it was most needed.

I closed my eyes in mourning. "I guess I could lose you."

We sped away, entering the sparser parts of town. Collecting our breaths, we listed out anyone who could help us.

"You think Charles can help? Like give a good word for us?" Tomas asked.

"Good words can only go so far now. We need to clear our name. We need proof that not even Hush can deny," I said.

"Yeah, but we can't do that if we don't have evidence. That's all at city hall," Tomas said.

All our normal avenues had dried up. We'd been working with the permission of everyone in Helford. They saw us in some ways as a public good, and we got leeway from it. We were allowed to act weird, skulk around, and ask questions. As soon as word got out that we were on the run from Hush, all of that would be down the drain.

I peered through the window into the passing trees. I was getting tired of being chased in forests, and we were set for another round of that. We'd been hounded by worse, but nothing as tenacious as Hush. We needed to think fast. Lucky for us, it was what I was best at.

"Park the car off the road, I think I have an idea," I said.

"And that is?" Tomas asked.

"Percival always shows when we're at our most desperate," I said.

"Yeah? It's sort of his MO," Tomas remarked.

"Then we'll make ourselves desperate. If he's behind this, then he'll show up."

Tomas didn't hesitate for a second. He parked the car on the mud-slicked forest floor. We got out, popped the hood, and grabbed our new-fangled suits.

Arriving on the scene, the deputies dug through the glove box, and scoured the floor. They pulled out police dogs, using them to sniff around for anything. They kept acting up when near the woods, but the deputies couldn't see anything.

"Probably just some animal," one deputy said.

What he didn't know was there was something. We were there the whole time, out in the open.

After watching what the Invisibeing's blood did to the things it covered, I thought it would be a good idea to keep a paint can's worth of the stuff. After a bit of experimenting, I went ahead and fashioned Tomas and me a set of invisibility suits. All I needed was goggles, boots, jumpsuits, gloves, and a ski mask to fully cover the body.

They were easy to put together, but had their own flaws baked in.

The biggest being how it did with water, which washed away the blood. The rain was light for now, but it wouldn't take long for the disguise to melt away.

We melded with the environment, traveling deeper into the forest. The cold was possessive, holding onto us every step of the way. A light drizzle collected on our suits, a rhythmic countdown signaling our vulnerable state. Unseen feet made deep imprints in the mud. Fall leaves turned wet and stuck to our invisible shoes.

Our goal was to hit a road a mile into the forest where we could back-track into town. We were lucky to not have the deputies breathing down our necks. That alone made the suits a roaring success. They did begin to fail on us.

The rain became less forgiving as we walked. White streaks of fabric peeked through the invisible veil. The blood trickled off our heads and down our bodies. We were fully in the open by the time we reached the road.

Both of us breathing heavily, Tomas asked, "How do you expect us to reach town on foot?"

"I don't," I said, holding out my thumb.

"If we're gonna do that, someone better show up soon or else we'll…" Tomas slowed his words as a limo appeared from a curve in the road and stopped beside us.

"All according to plan," I said.

"How do you always manage to blur the lines between luck and skill?" Tomas asked.

Before I could answer, the backseat window of the limo rolled down. It was Percival Maelie, along with his squad of wax mobsters.

"Mr. Whitlock, it's good to see you two in one piece," Percival said.

I rested my hand on my holster while Tomas grabbed his magic gloves.

"You got a good reason for us not to blast you into next week?" I said, withholding the fact that my gun would do nothing to him.

"Because you need a place to hide, and I need your help," Percival said.

That last part gave me pause. "Explain,"

Percival sighed, saying, "We don't have room to explain. You just need to weigh which is more important: the people in city hall, or your hatred of me."

Tomas stepped beside me, and whispered, "What should we do?"

"Well there's nothing he gets in killing us," I said.

"That sure is comforting," Tomas said.

Tomas and I opened the car doors and sat in the seats left vacant for us. I was already beginning to regret my decision when Percival Maelie cracked out his signature smile.

"Great. We have much to talk about."

The back door shut, and the car began to move.

Wherever it was going, I couldn't say.

# CHAPTER 23

He took us to an abandoned theater. It was called the "Night House," the letters up front having become missing or lopsided with time. The parking lot was empty, the wind sliding through with little resistance. Stained movie posters in plastic displays worked as a runway towards the entrance.

Inside, star-littered black carpet had become loose patches of frayed string. Obstacles were laid before us by past visitors. Trash cans, shattered glass, and vandalized popcorn machines peppered the floor. Graffiti murals reached across the walls, full to the brim with crude symbols and phallic objects.

Things started to look better when Percival took us up to his room, which was set up in one of the theater projector booths. The shabby carpets were replaced by fine rugs made with intricate Egyptian patterns. Where one of the projectors would have been was instead a desk with piles of notes and books. A wax mobster stood blocking what the notes read. At the corner of the booth was a pristine chair, along with a wood coffee table and a less fancy futon.

"You two make yourselves comfortable while one of my guards makes us tea." Percival said.

He sat at the chair, while a guard began to play music with an antique violin. Tomas and I looked at each other confused, but nonetheless sat down on the futon.

"Homey place you got here," I said.

"It's one of the pieces of Helford that died when I left office. Needless to say there are many more like it. I believe this one was property of the Orlando Corporation," Percival said.

"Weird way to be emotionally connected to something," I remarked.

"It makes more sense when you come to understand why. This was Helford's future, and my legacy. It was tragic really, a few signatures and we would have had true progress."

"You call selling the town progress?" Tomas said.

"When in good hands, yes. Our world is on an ever changing course, one in which animals eat animals. You need powerful men to steer towns like this from self-cannibalism." Percival said.

"Yeah, powerful men would have had a field day here," I said.

"You of all people should understand, Mr. Whitlock. Your uncle worked hard to keep this town from dying, and they thanked him with isolation. What makes you think they won't do the same to you?" Percival said.

"What makes you think ruling them like kings would change that?" I said.

Percival sighed, saying, "When the news came out about my occult rituals, I knew it was your uncle who told them. I told him what I had planned for Helford, and he reacted the same way you do now."

The room went silent for a second, Tomas breaking it with small talk.

"You know we actually met Mr. Orlando before," Tomas said.

Percival bit the bait and asked, "And how did that go?"

"Well, we dropped his ceiling and took his stuff," Tomas said.

Percival struggled to give a clever response, only giving a content "Hm."

As I thought through my decisions, one of the mobsters came around with tea. Tomas and Percival got a cup while I abstained.

"Forgive me but last time we had tea with you, it didn't end so well," I said. Tomas nodded in agreement.

"We have had a troubled history haven't we?" Percival smiled with a touch of nostalgia.
"But we'll have to put that aside for once."

Something felt off. Percival was too welcoming, too willing to let us talk. He wasn't someone okay with letting a moment pass. That is, unless there was something to gain from it.

I needed to cut at his plan and get to the point.

"Was what happened at city hall your dirty work?" I asked.

"I hoped you'd know better than to think that, Mr. Whitlock," Percival said.

"Oh, forgive us for thinking you weren't above that after all this time," Tomas said.

Percival looked almost hurt by that statement. "True power is knowing when violence is necessary. That's what separates kings from brutes. Believe me, I have no desire to commit needless violence, especially when it involves my own sister."

That was hard to argue against. Percival was willing to turn a blind eye and work with monsters, but he wasn't wild like a lot of them were. He was sophisticated, and I couldn't tell whether that was better or worse.

"If it wasn't our resident bad guy, then who was it?" I said.

Percival breathed in the steam, taking a sip of his tea. "That's what I need you two for."

"You do?" Tomas and I said.

"As I said before, my sister is involved, and I'm not someone who is willing to let slights like that go unpunished. Besides, allowing random acts of violence to happen in Helford will only end up harming my future plans," Percival said.

"Glad you found a way for acts of empathy to still benefit your master plan," I said.

"Keep biting back all you want, Mr. Whitlock, but it only hurts you, not me," Percival said, taking a smug sip of tea.

I could feel my annoyance bubble up, but he was right. We somehow had less wiggle room than the time we fought a giant lizard.

"Fine, let's start with what you know," I said.

Percival snapped his finger. In response, one of the guards retrieved a cardboard box wrapped in purple paper. It was decorated in the same way as the letter we had received.

"This box was left open at the mayor's moments before you two arrived," Percival said.

"Can I take a look at it?" I asked.

Percival nodded, sliding the box across the table to me. I ran my hands over it, a prickling feeling running up the lower part of my spine. I recognized the feeling instantly. Ever since we fought Basket Case, I'd been practicing with Tomas to better detect surface-level magic. Tomas was still leagues above me. He practiced his nerves enough to be able to identify magic off of the air alone.

Giving it over to Tomas, he held the box up to get a better look at it. Getting close enough to lick it, Tomas squinted his eyes in concentration.

"Yep, that's your problem," Tomas said.

"The heck is that supposed to mean?" I said.

Tomas opened the box, gesturing at the inside. "You see, the inside and outside of the box have two entirely different kinds of magic. The inside is absolutely coated in glamour, while the outside has a special kind of protective wrapping."

Tomas ripped the paper wrapping away. Hidden underneath were ornate symbols beyond my understanding.

Tomas nodded the same way someone does when looking over a car.

"There we go, that's what we're looking for. The protective symbols were being used to keep something in until someone opened it," Tomas said.

"So it's sort of like a Pandora's box, you open it up and it releases some dangerous spell," I said.

"Exactly, though it's a bit crude," Tomas explained. "Anyone worth their stuff would just send the spell using a specially-designed ritual. Doing it like this is like having a gun and throwing bullets at the person instead of shooting them."

"Well, it worked, because it got a building full of people cursed," I said.

"That's what's confusing me. This spell was powerful, and beyond anything a novice could do," Tomas said.

"So we need to find someone who has the talent to do this but isn't skilled enough to do something more efficient," I said.

"Doesn't really narrow it down, does it?" Tomas said.

As we talked, Percival watched us. He didn't seem to be impressed with us, but he wasn't uninterested either. Telling from Charles's stories, there was more to the supernatural outside of Helford. It wasn't crazy to assume that Percival was more familiar with that wider world than we were.

I asked Tomas to have one last look over the box. I peered in, searching for anything physical. Something was missing, and I couldn't find it off of feeling alone. I noticed that one of the inner folds stood higher than the other.

Pulling the fold exposed what looked to be a fake eyelash. Something felt off about it. It wasn't realistic, looking more like snipped and frayed plastic rather than something used for cosmetics. It was also child sized, making it even harder to imagine someone wearing them. That is except for one person.

I showed the lash to Tomas. "You recognize it from anything?"

Tomas pursed his lips. "Looks like one of Matilda's lashes."

"Exactly, and you know who else had dolls?" I asked.

A bit of color left Tomas's face "But there's no way."

"Think about it: a crude but powerful glamour spell goes off in city hall. Glamour was basically her whole thing," I said.

"Yeah, but we also left her six feet under, flailing around completely blind. Not even she can recover from that," Tomas said.

Basket Case was powerful, but she wasn't invincible. Everything before pointed to her being dead. If she was alive, she would have already made that more than clear to us. She was never complicated, and her kind of revenge wouldn't be either.

Staring at one of the animated mobsters, I came to one realization.

"Her dolls," I said under my breath.

"Her what?" Tomas said.

"Just before we escaped, I saw her dolls surrounding her. Maybe her last act was to save them. It would make sense, she never left those things alone." I then asked Percival, "Do things animated by life dust become attached to their owners?"

"It depends on how long the owner had the item. The longer the person owns the item, the more advanced the item's sentience is," Percival said.

"If that's true, why is Matilda so sentient?" Tomas asked.

"It's also determined by how the person got the item. You bought her from the store, meaning the ownership was more legitimate. Though that also made her more childlike since you had gotten her so recently," Percival explained.

"Is that why you stole the mobsters? So their sentience wouldn't get in the way?" I said.

"I needed loyal machines, not children," Percival said.

"Yeesh," Tomas let out.

"So that's it, isn't it? Basket Case's dolls survived and have been planning their revenge since then," Tomas said.

"It'd explain why it took them so long. It can't be easy walking around as a squad of living dolls," I said.

"There's one hole in that theory," Percival added. "Things animated by life dust can't do magic."

"They might be working with someone," I said.

"We have made a lot of enemies." Tomas pointed to Percival. "Case in point."

I pressed myself into the chair. We'd been moving all day, and I could feel my bones pulling down on me. I gave the lash a look over before handing it to Tomas.

"Well… there's only one way to find out. Think you can track that?" I asked Tomas.

"In theory, yeah," Tomas responded.

I picked myself up, my brain force-fed a hefty dose of determination. "Then let's get to work. If we finish this quickly, we might be home by midnight."

Even the wax mobsters looked at me with a bit of doubt on that one.

# CHAPTER 24

It was a bit nostalgic chasing those dolls down again. All the monsters we fought, all the mysteries we solved, all led up to us riding in a limo with a squad of wax figures and my worst enemy by our side.

The lash guided us. Tied to a pendulum, it swung in the direction we needed to go to find the dolls. Tomas was pretty rusty with the spell and had to relearn a lot of it. It was sort of a last resort for us, since it required a piece of the thing we were tracking. It took work to get something like that, which on our end mostly meant good sleuthing.

As Tomas guided the wax driver in the right direction, I prepared with the rest of the mobsters. The wax figures loaded Tommy guns, pistols and shotguns. A few even sharpened knives, polishing them with their own skin.

I loaded my revolver and made sure I had multiple speed loaders on hand. My ax was as sharp as I could make it and placed snugly in my utility belt.

It had gotten dark, the window's tint making it so the only thing I could see was my reflection. We were deep in the bad parts of Helford, as the potholes reminded us every few feet.

Unlike everyone else, Percival wasn't preparing. He was unarmed, hands clasped together in a pose expected from an egomaniac. He had a quaint smile. It was so unbecoming of a face so used to smug ones. I could feel him devising some plan to screw us over.

"What do you expect to happen when this all turns over?" I asked him.

Broken from his trance, Percival said, "Not a good question to be asking your ally, is it?"

"No, but it's a good one for you," I said.

Percival's smug smile returned. "You really think I'm going to kill you?"

"It wouldn't be out of character for you to be lying to us."

Percival looked at me like I was joking. "Mr. Whitlock, I've been honest since the moment we met."

The limo came to a stop.

"We're here," Tomas said.

We had stopped at what looked to be an abandoned factory. Rusted walls and broken windows held up a haunting silhouette. Everyone got out, splitting into two groups.

"How much do you wanna bet it's booby trapped?" I asked Tomas.

"Dude, is that even a question at this point," Tomas responded.

"How do you want to do this?" Percival asked.

"We'll stick together for now. No point in splitting up when we don't know what we're in for," I said.

Percival agreed. We slipped in through one of the fire exits. The ground floor was full of old textile equipment. Machines built to process and move strings were left to break with time. The place felt too empty for comfort. Footsteps echoed on the smooth concrete floor.

Signs showed something was amongst the garbage. Equipment had been dragged around and stacked, a maze designed to funnel us into unknown dangers.

One danger revealed itself a quarter of the way through. Soft footsteps rattled above us and went silent. There was a sudden snap, followed by the skipping of a fast spinning pulley. Tracing the sound, I tackled Percival out of the way of the oncoming trap. A wood board fixed with an array of knives shattered on the ground, clattering in an orchestra of sound.

Tomas went to help but was stopped when a web of string lassoed around him. The string pulled at him, bringing him towards the gnashing maw of textile machinery. Tomas called out for help, and I responded. I took out my ax and threw it at the coalescing string. Tomas used his strength to break free from the rest of the fraying strands. Tomas fell on his knees, checking his body for missing limbs.

"Holy crap," Tomas said through heavy breathing.

As we all recovered, the factory's intercom beeped to life. Screeching through broken static was the artificial voice of a text-to-speech program.

"It's tragic…to see you still breathing… murderer," the voice echoed.

"If you think that's bad, then you're not ready for what's going to come next," Percival announced.

"Though I'm sure you were expecting us to get past that, weren't you?" I added.

"Expect it? No… We were betting on it," the voice finished.

Tomas looked at me with a newfound rush of determination.

He slid the ax over to me and said, "Let's clear this place."

We moved forward, keeping low to avoid our heads getting clipped by booby traps. Turning a corner in the maze, I stopped everyone, making sure to peek over for any dangers. Leaning out of the corner, I squinted to spot anything in the darkness. Amongst that blackness was the slight sheen of two porcelain heads. Hearing the sound of movement, I flew back behind the corner's safety.

Gliding past the space I had been milliseconds before, a crossbow bolt planted itself deep in a box of fabrics. Sound came through the darkness as the two dolls strained to crank back their crossbow for another bolt.

"Tomas, break and aim on three," I said.

Tomas nodded in agreement. Getting into positions, I counted down to three. Hitting three, we lunged from the corner. Tomas threw out his arm, concentrating his magic on a single point of the crossbow's string. Heat collected and cooked through it, causing it to snap. The bolt made a pitiful launch, landing only a few feet away. Confused with what just happened, the dolls continued cranking in vain. I didn't give them a second to react, firing two shots into the darkness. The shattered porcelain clattered on the concrete floor. For a second, the place was in mournful silence.

"Clear," I said.

We kept moving through the maze, avoiding traps and taking out the dolls who set them off. The dolls verged on the suicidal, doing anything they could to kill us. One even shattered itself to activate a trap by falling on it. They hated us with every fabric of their short existence. We killed their mother, and it was now their job to even the score.

Reaching the end of the maze, we exited the main work floor of the factory and entered its individual office area. There were even more areas to clear, and more places for the dolls to set up booby traps.

"We're getting nowhere clearing these rooms one by one," I said.

Percival stepped to the front, arms behind his back. "Guards, do what I made you for."

The wax mobsters marched forward, banding into groups of three. The groups busted down each office door and flowed into the rooms. Their guns clacked like typewriters, silencing the rooms with sounds of death.

Percival walked down the hall and up the stairs, confident with the security of his wax guards. We chased after him, not wanting to be caught with our pants down.

The second floor was the same as the office floor below. The manager's office stood proud at the end of the hall. At the middle of the hall was an open office door emanating with green light.

We stopped at the door. Inside was a smoke filled cauldron along with shelves filled with glowing potions. Percival grinned like this was the room he was hoping to find all along. I stopped him before he could take a step inside.

"No way I'm leaving you alone with this stuff," I said.

"And why is that?" Percival asked.

"Because I know you," I responded.

"Mr. Whitlock, there are still threats in the building as we speak, ones that you are best equipped at dealing with. Do your job and I'll do mine," Percival said.

"Like you even know what we're looking for," I said.

"Unlike you, I know value when I see it," Percival smiled.

Before I could argue further, Tomas placed his hand on my shoulder. His eyes told me we needed to keep going and pick our battles. I swallowed that part of me that wanted to scream no. Percival entered the cauldron room, leaving us to deal with the manager's office.

Tomas and I nodded in unison and approached the door. Busting it down, we entered, ready to fight.

The manager's room was expansive with large windows made to look over the whole work room. Files stuffed in the room's corners cooked under heat and mold. A mahogany desk lay in the middle with a tall office chair turned away from us towards the window.

Sitting on the desk was a porcelain doll. Stuffed hands typed away on a keyboard, plastic amber eyes reflected a white ocean of words.

"It's over, doll, there's nowhere else left to go," I said.

"Not quite," the text-to-speech responded. "There are more tricks I've yet to use."

"You better start typing up why, fast," I said.

"With you leaving our mother for dead, we were forced to adapt. Now we have you where we need you. To serve our justice and your doom," the doll said.

"Those are some poetic words for someone outnumbered two to one," I said.

"And here I thought you knew how to count," a familiar voice said.

The office chair swung around, revealing the schlubby cupid-winged man who sat in it. It was Trellis, and boy, had he let himself go. His blonde hair and goatee had grown shaggy. He wore the same clothes he did in Revival Fest, but they looked a lot less flattering in the place he was now.

"What the hell? Trellis?" I said.

"You remember! I guess it's the best you can do after ruining my life," Trellis said, bug-eyed.

"Ruined your life? What are you talking about? We beat you at a game of cornhole," I said.

"Oh you did way more than that. Before you guys showed up, I had everything. Everyone loved me. They trusted me as the only one who could speak Revival Fest's wisdom. I got all the love I could ever need. I feasted on every single bit of it. Then you arrived. Just imagine, you're chilling, and then some newbie shows up, calls you a liar, and then on their first day connects to Revival Fest. What does that do to someone's reputation? What does that do to me? I lost everything and it's all your fault."

My mind built up a list of theatrical comebacks. The kind of speeches super heroes would use against their greatest nemesis. Yet they all fell flat on arrival. No matter how hard I tried, I couldn't find the will to care about his needless spiraling.

"I gotta give it to you, Trellis. You did something really interesting with this little monster team up, but that's the scariest thing about you right now," I said.

"Whatever, man. I'm having your head on a spike whether you think I'm a joke or not." Trellis said.

"That makes two of us," another voice said behind us.

We did a slow turn around, unsure who exactly said it.

"Hush?" I said.

The office went silent. Hush's badge shone in the flickering sodium lights. His calloused hands dug into khaki pants. His cheeks strained to hold up his devious grin. He stood sure of what was going to happen next.

"What are you doing here?" I said.

"Where's all the other deputies?" Tomas added.

"How 'bout we put a hold on all the questions and make this quick."

In the dim light, his skin shifted to a dark green hue. Rough scales grew like hairs standing on end. Claws pushed out a foot from his nails, his fingers extending with them. He offered his hand, his smile now topped off with ferocious fangs.

Tomas and I went quiet. I'd been praying we'd never meet that thing again. The same thing that attacked Tomas and me at the secret society lodge. The same thing that we couldn't beat before.

"You were the Monitor this whole time?" I said.

"Aw, I'm touched. You gave me a little name," Hush said, grinning.

"But why? How?" Tomas said.

"You guys have yapped enough for one day. All you need to know is that some people need secrets hidden in Helford, and because of that you two are too nosey to keep alive." Hush explained.

"Of all the people who decided to be quick with monologuing, it had to be the one I had the most questions about?" I said.

"We don't always get what we want. Anyways, I'm gonna—"

Before Hush could finish his sentence, Tomas threw a kinetic blast of magical energy. Hush's flailing body whizzed down the hall and smashed into the stairwell's wall. Dust and shards ruptured from the concrete.

"Damn, Tomas," I said.

"Save it, let's bolt," Tomas yelled back.

Hush survived worse attacks, so it wasn't going to take long for him to get back up. I looked around the manager's office for any escape routes. The only exit out was the one we had thrown Hush at.

We needed to make a new way out. Past the manager's viewing windows was a rusted catwalk. The breaking walkway led from one end of the work area to the other.

"Follow my lead," I said to Tomas, running towards the windows.

"Oh no you don't," Trellis said, getting in the way.

Fully out of patience, I socked Trellis square in the jaw. He crumpled like a garbage bag, his body falling limp onto the floor. I threw the office chair through the windows, shattering the glass. We leapt out onto the walkway, running across it towards the entrance.

"Crap, there aren't any steps leading down," I said as we ran.

Tomas stopped me and wrapped one of his arms around my waist. I looked at him both confused and strangely intrigued.

With a confident grin, Tomas said, "Hold on tight."

Red strands flickered around the cables in front of us suspending the catwalk. The cables screeched and roared, the wires becoming a bright red. The cables snapped, causing the catwalk to slant downwards towards the front entrance. Wind rushed past us as we slid down the catwalk and onto a smooth concrete floor.

On the ground I said, "You always find a way to surprise me."

"It's what I live for," Tomas said.

We got hit with more problems outside. The issue was, if we left with the limo, we'd be leaving without the guy who owned it. I hated Percival, but I wasn't leaving him to get gutted by the big komodo dragon who was after us. If we were escaping, we needed to draw the lizard away without nabbing Percival's limo.

Good thing for us, there was a new car outside. Despite being able to clock speeds unmatched by any human on earth, Hush wasn't keen on going all over Helford by foot. His car sat outside, ready to be taken.

As we ran to the car, Tomas suggested, "I can use magic to break the locks open."

"Save it for the hotwiring," I said, shattering the front window with the back of my ax.

I unlocked the door, letting Tomas do the rest. Ten painstaking seconds passed and the car hummed to life. Before I knew it, we were pressed in our seats, leaving smoke and skid marks behind us.

We scampered to our next destination, our house. There was no next time with these guys. They wouldn't stop hunting us till we slept in shallow graves. We were ending this tonight, and I had a plan.

# CHAPTER 25

Wind rushed through the Sheriff's broken window, filling our lungs with delicious air. Tomas drove while I gave a short call to Matilda back at home.

"You need to listen to me carefully, Matilda. Go get the dry ice and leave it outside in bins. After you do that, don't leave the house for any reason, okay? Bye." I finished the call, breathing a sigh of relief.

"You really think it's gonna work?" Tomas asked.

"Theoretically," I said.

"Oh, so like our other plans," Tomas said.

The streets were quiet, like the whole town had been closed off for this very event. We roared down the roads in a stolen car to have a final battle in our front yard.

Sometimes life can be a bit heavy-handed with making things interesting.

Anxiety's cold warmth pulsed up my back. Considering how it was last time with the Monitor, it wouldn't be an easy fight. We couldn't run like we had before.

"Tomas?"

"Yeah, Jonathan?"

"What are we going to do after this?" I asked.

"Rest for a few days, probably," Tomas said.

"No, I mean after even that. What do we do after all this…" I tried to look for some sophisticated way to describe it but couldn't. "Craziness. Can we really get back to our usual thing?"

Tomas shrugged. "It's crazier to think this wouldn't happen eventually. I don't have a reference for this. I used to move carts around before I met you."

I laughed. "You must be wishing to have that back now."

"Hm, not really. It sucked, and I begged every day for something to change. I don't need to ask for that anymore. It's kinda nice. I like being around you," Tomas said.

It might have been the adrenaline, but my chest felt light. I had one question to ask. It felt scarier to ask than any of the monsters and creatures we'd fought before.

"Tomas, maybe sometime this week or something. Would you like to go on a—"

"Wait." Tomas stopped me. "Do you hear something?"

We went silent. It was hard to hear through the wind and engine. I looked around for what it could be. That's when I saw the bright light in the rearview mirror.

We rocked forward, my face stopping an inch from the dashboard. Something had hit us from behind.

It was a car. The thing was beaten to high hell, looking like it had seen a decade in a warzone. Trash filled the back seats. The smell of weed was so palpable not even the wind could push it away. Looking up at the dash, I saw who was driving that rotting lemon. It was Trellis, and he wasn't alone.

Atop the vehicle, a pair of eyes were lit by the raging lights. Dark massive claws gripped to the hood of the car like a cat. Hush readied himself and pounced.

"Push the gas! Now!" I shouted.

Tomas did, but it was too late. Our car bounced. Extra weight had landed onto the back of our vehicle. I swung around and fired a hail of shots. The glass shattered, but nothing was hit.

Trellis steered his car out of the way of any more shots, and Hush was nowhere to be found. We didn't have to wonder where he was for long. Long nails stabbed into the top of the car, making a shrieking pop.

I tried to aim my gun but was thrown off by Trellis slamming his car into the side of ours. He kept at it, pushing us closer to the edge of the road. We needed to buy more time, but these freaks wouldn't give it to us. It was time to divide and conquer.

I aimed my gun at Trellis, using Tomas's arm as a stabilizer. I waited for Trellis to pull his car back and fired. The bullet grazed one of Trellis' arms. Blood splattered the windows, and Trellis yelped. He'd been a lover all his life and handled a wound as well as anyone did with that lifestyle. He swerved side to side. Losing control, he rolled off the road and got stuck in a ditch.

Hush would be harder, and he made that clear when he started carving through the car. He pulled metal away like wrapping paper. He dived in to grab his meaty gifts. Slipping my legs to the driver side, I pressed on the gas with one foot and pushed Tomas's underseat bar with the other. His seat went back, away from the wheel, and Hush snapped at the air. Before he had the chance to bring his head back up, I gave the steering wheel a hard smack with my ax. The airbag exploded, the kinetic force blasting Hush square in the jaw. He struggled to get himself out of the fabric, not helped by the fact that he was stunned. I was shocked it worked. It was a huge reminder for me to get my own airbags checked.

I kept the steering wheel straight long enough for Tomas to retake it. Our house was now within throwing distance from us. We just needed to stop, which was impossible with a lizard monster ready to carve us up at a moment's notice. Hush pulled his head out and unlatched one of his hands from the car. He steadied his hand to make a clean stab at one of us.

What happened next was a bit confusing on Tomas's end. Maybe he wanted to throw off Hush. Maybe he thought a quick stop could give us a chance to escape. It was probably a mix of both. In practice, he did a hard twist with the steering wheel and made the car flip.

We tumbled through our yard, managing to eke out three spins before landing upside down. Debris and my hand ax swirled inside the car, testing our luck in the car crash version of Russian roulette.

Hush got a similar fate. He was thrown off on the first tumble. His body landed on the magic barrier blocking the home. For the first time ever, I saw what the barrier did. It cooked the surface of Hush's back flesh. Green bolts hopped up his back like skipping stones. His body was then repelled, throwing him a few feet away.

We laid suspended from our seatbelts, covered in aching cuts and bruises. I unlatched the seatbelt, and gravity punished me. I landed on a bed of broken glass, my uncle's jacket taking the brunt of the damage.

I pulled Tomas out with me, my body begging for bandaids and a comfy bed. Hush did just as well as us. The three of us recovered at around the same pace.

Matilda had done as I asked. Surrounding us were plastic bins full of dry ice. Carbon dioxide erupted out and flowed to the ground. A strange atmosphere formed. It felt present. Air left our lungs, warmth mixing with cold. Our hair stood up in response to tingling nerves. We were tired enemies ready to make a new world in one bout of violence. It may have been the only thing we could agree on.

"Are you ready or not?" I asked Hush.

His shoulders narrowed down and lowered into a predator's stance. He clenched and released his hands in a rhythmic pattern.

I brought my ax and gun to bear. "Thought so."

Tomas stepped back, concentrating magic as per our plan. I stepped forward, and Hush presented his claws.

Hush charged me, his lizard claws slicing through the air. I first used my pistol, firing a few shots at his legs. He was unaffected, his adrenaline working overtime to hold down the pain of the bouncing shots.

Getting close, Hush made a fan-like swing. I avoided it but was nicked on the cheek. I stumbled back, and Hush pursued me.

What made Hush different from my other opponents was that he knew how to keep his priorities straight. Instead of attacking me again with his claws, he shoulder checked me. Once I was flat on the ground, he rushed for Tomas.

Hush had seen enough from Tomas to know that he was a heavy hitter when left alone. I could be dealt with later.

I looked for anything to exploit on Hush. All across Hush's back was skin made raw from hitting the wall. I had run out of bullets, so I grabbed my ax and threw it into his back. The ax planted itself deep in. Hush hissed in pain, blood gushing from the wound.

It slowed Hush down, but a few more steps would put him in range of hitting Tomas. I got up, sprinting towards Hush. I tackled him from behind, attempting to hold him down. My hand held tight on the ax, and it ripped out of him as he threw me off. He shrieked from the opening wound.

He diverted his attention to me, sending a flurry of attacks at me. The jacket kept any of the attacks from carving through me, but it didn't help with blunting the force of the attacks. I was in a bad shape, and one more attack would knock me down for good.

Hush swung at me, and I tried to block the attack with my own. My ax went down at the claws and shattered them like ice. The fingers of one of his hands fell over into pieces of frozen meat. We stood there confused.

Hush went for another attack, but I was ready for it. More frozen fingers fell to the ground. Hush stepped back. Carbon dioxide shot up from the bins like a violent volcano. The plan worked, and a big grin began to form on my face.

"Surprised? I'll pay the favor and make this explanation simple too. Energy can't be created or destroyed, and that goes for heat too. Right now we're using magic and all this dry ice to help transfer heat out of you, and boy can this stuff get cold."

Hush attempted to throw more attacks, fingers be damned. The colder he got, the slower he was becoming. His cold-blooded body struggled to survive under such intense colds. More of him got lopped off with each cut.

"You wanna know what your biggest mistake was?" I asked.

I brought my ax down. Steel carved down a brittle clavicle and into the left lung. Shock filled Hush's eyes as his body turned completely frozen.

"It's that you gave us time to prepare," I said, kicking his cold dead body onto the ground.

Seeing each other across the settling fog, Tomas and I both felt a rush of relief. We took out Hush. The threat was settled.

"Dude, we did it!" Tomas cheered.

"We did!" I cheered back.

Tomas ran over to give me one big hug, but then something hit him. A purple bolt of smoke-like glitter engulfed his head. All at once, the glitter rushed through his mouth, ears, and face. Tomas staggered and fell. Drowsy eyes plunged into deep sleep.

"Tomas!" I panted.

I ran over to him, kneeling down close. I tried in vain to shake him awake. Confusion and fear dragged me from my fighting spirit. All I could think of was how to wake him up.

Trellis cackled.

"See! You thought you got rid of me with that little trick, but no! I can fly, you stupid idiot. I don't need anyone… anyone!" Trellis rambled.

I couldn't concentrate on him. I just wanted Tomas to be okay. I didn't want what happened to everyone else to happen to him.

"When all this is over, I'll be on top. I could make this whole place a party for the rest of time."

I turned around to face what would happen next. Trellis lifted his arm defiantly, collecting glitter in the palm of his hand.

"How's that for a party foul—"

A string of gunshots rang through the forest. Five shots passed through his back and out his chest. Trellis stood still. He stared at his bloody hands in disbelief. He tried to take a few steps forward, unable to process the new wounds. His body soon recognized reality. He fell to his knees, and his bleeding chest became acquainted with the cold dirt.

The one who pulled the trigger: Percival Maelie.

Percival held his stance, his gun smoking. He handed the pistol back to one of his wax guards.

"And that's the end of our truce," Percival said.

He stood over me, hands in pockets.

"So that fool got to him?" Percival asked.

The words left through my struggling tears, ending in meek silence. Percival understood.

"A tragedy, but one I have the cure for."

Percival pulled a potion full of a glowing purple liquid from his suit pocket.

"I found the cure while you had them distracted. I'll give it to you, but not for free. Invite me to the house, and you can have the potion," Percival said.

"No… I can't… you won't," I said.

"Oh Whitlock, when have I ever lied to you?"

I held Tomas tight, holding him as I cried. I could feel his chest move like a ship amongst the waves. I couldn't let this happen, leave him in this state.

"Fine… You're invited… Just go," I said.

Percival sighed, all his years of work coming to an end. He laid the cure beside me, patting me on the shoulder.

"Take your time," Percival said.

Two guards stayed beside us while Percival and the rest entered the house. He did what he promised, and he got everything because of it. I held onto the cure and Tomas for a bit longer. I didn't want to face what I did, and what would come from it. I just wanted him back and awake. I wanted to talk to him again and make the air no longer hollow.

# CHAPTER 26

It took three drops. Strange glittering purple fell in, and his eyes rose like the sun. We were still outside, Tomas's cold breath gaining strength as he awoke. He woke up like he would any other morning.

Stretching his arms, Tomas asked, "What happened?"

I didn't say anything. I hugged him tight, tears soaking his jacket. Tomas tensed, surprised, still in a sleepy haze. He loosened, patting my back.

"Where are we? Did you leave me on the ground?" Tomas said.

I wiped away tears. "No, you haven't been out for long."

Tomas eyed my tired face and drying tears, and the two guards hovering over us. "What the hell?"

Noticing the now open door to our house, he realized what happened.

"Oh no... dude, we gotta go and stop him," Tomas said.

"And do what? He won, and there's nothing we can do. We don't even know what he's after," I said.

"How did he get in?" Tomas asked.

"Well—"

All the windows in the house turned a bright green. The middle of our roof exploded out, releasing a cacophony of color. It sounded like a rushing river, constant and deafening. Plants and moss took over, green spreading at an infectious speed. Even the empty shells of the wax mobsters looked in awe of the sight.

I could taste the magic coming off of it. Strange creatures flew out and glided down like dandelions. Some were unrecognizable to me even after a year of studying the occult.

"It was the only way I could save you and everyone else," I said.

"I… I'm sorry, this is a lot to wake up to… thank you for doing that for me," Tomas said.

I did my best to smile through red eyes. The moment passed and Matilda appeared from the house. She ran with her little legs and tackled us in a warm embrace.

"We're okay," I whispered over and over.

"We're just happy you're safe," Tomas said.

Matilda pulled her white board and drew a little heart.

"Help soon," she wrote.

"It's okay, there's not really anything else we can do," I said.

My heart sank a bit saying it. There wasn't a lot we could do while under gunpoint by two wax guards. I doubt they'd be fooled as easily by our old tricks.

Matilda shook her head, and wrote "No, got help!"

"Whose help did you get?" Tomas said.

A pitch black muscle car tore into our driveway. It swerved to a stop parallel to the guards. The window rolled down, and two gunshots went off. Two wax heads exploded, their headless bodies flopping onto the ground. The car door swung open, revealing Charles Damien Nightwood. Charles marched over, pulling us both up by our arms.

"I'm starting to think you guys are asking to be rescued," Charles smiled.

"It's not our fault this is how we spend our afternoons," Tomas joked.

"Maybe you guys gotta do dinner and a movie sometime, change things up," Charles said.

"We'll think about it. How did you get here so quickly? I thought you left." I asked.

"I was about to. Then I got a call from that little hero over there. It took a while to read all she wrote on Facetime, but she got me caught up. Seems like a lot has changed since she wrote that," Charles said.

"It's Percival again, He went in and all this happened," I said.

"He opened the door in the basement didn't he?" Charles asked.

"You know what's in there?" I asked.

Charles shook his head "It's one of the secrets Kasper chose to keep from me. All I can tell you is that whatever is in there is not good news."

"It does seem to be throwing up a lot of stuff," Tomas said.

"How are we going to stop him?" I said.

"Someone might have to chase after him, but there's a problem with that. Whoever goes, others will need to stay to make sure nothing dangerous gets out," Charles said.

"So one of us has to go?" Tomas said.

Charles nodded. Everyone stood silent. None of us knew what was going on, and that made this whole situation twice as dangerous. I stepped forward.

"I'll do it," I said.

"What?" Tomas exclaimed.

"You sure about this?" Charles asked.

"Percival has been my problem since I met him. If there's anyone that knows him, it's me," I said.

Charles held no doubt about me in his eyes. It was a trusting intensity that I'd never seen before.

"Then it's settled. You go in while we cover you and the entrance. Does that work?"

Tomas looked between us and nodded in agreement.

"Then break," Charles clapped.

We ran into the house. The inside was covered floor to ceiling with monsters. Most parted to let us through, while others went for the kill. We hacked, burned, and cut our way to the basement. Matilda helped as well, jumping on and distracting the monsters attacking us.

We got into the basement. Mushrooms cracked through the wood floor. Centipedes moved between the crevices, and spores filled the room. Strange roses hummed and whispered as we stepped by them. Wind pressed through the open door, the supernatural flying through it like rapids.

Tomas and Charles stood guard, gloves and shotgun at the ready. I was about to step through but stopped. I needed to get something off my chest.

"Tomas."

"Yeah?"

"If—If I get out of this in one piece, you wanna get something nice to eat? Just you and me," I said

"Oh—I um… Yes… I would love that," Tomas responded.

Charles gave me an approving thumbs up. My heart got just a bit lighter, and I felt less scared. I continued forward when Tomas stopped me.

"Hey… You owe me a date now, so don't die on me, okay?"

"The whole world could end and I'd still go," I smiled.

I ran forward and fell straight into a new world.

# CHAPTER 27

In the year I'd been a monster hunter, none of it could have prepared me for this.

It was like a jungle cathedral. Supersized plants reached tens of stories high towards an earthen ceiling. Car-sized mushrooms collected on the landscape in heavy splotches. The air was different here, making me want to dance and rest at the same time. It felt like chains I never noticed before had slid off me all at once.

Soft music made loud echoes through the caverns like whales singing in a vast sea. Everything had the plastic sheen of a lawn decoration. This world mixed both natural and unnatural in ways outside my understanding.

I almost got lost in the wonder of it all until I collected myself and remembered why I was there. I'd seen

Revival Fest before, so I was somewhat inoculated to the otherworldly feelings this place gave out. To think, this frenzied mess of contradictions had been marinating under my house this entire time.

I explored the area, looking for tracks that I could follow. I stopped looking after noticing the ground around this area was semi-elastic. Footprints disappeared a minute after they were made.

I then noticed a group of gnomes chilling by a mushroom. They smoked on cattails, blowing the smoke in each other's faces. They wore shades with dark crazed hair and black clothes. One of them played bongos. They looked like the people who went to open mic nights at coffee shops. Tomas and I had a bad experience at one of those. It wasn't our fault the poetry was kind of funny.

I really didn't want to talk to them. I also had no other choice.

Approaching them, I asked, "Hey, uh… Have you seen this guy? He's this tall? Wears a suit? Looks like he eats crap for breakfast?"

"Oh yeah, him! He's going down towards the Lotus Fields. Asked us about it at gunpoint. You can't miss it. Just pass the Root Maze, and avoid the Forest of the Dead," the gnome with the beret and goatee said.

"The *what*?"

"You'll know it when you see it," he waved.

Needing more context, I asked, "So what is this place?"

"You mean the Faerie Mound in general or just the part you're in right now?" he said.

"Faerie Mound?"

"Both then. Right now you're in the Yard Jungle. It's pretty nice. It makes up most of the Mound. It's the least dangerous place here," he said.

"So it's safe?"

"I didn't say that. But yeah, you're in a Faerie Mound. A biome for all sorts of strange and whimsical beasties to live. Well, strange and whimsical to you. For me it's just Tuesday," he said.

"And you're?"

"Name's Blueberry, and this is my crew. We're a bit chiller than the other people you meet around here," Blueberry said.

"Anyone in particular I need to watch out for?" I asked.

"Hm, anything that breathes really. Just respect others and you'll be fine. Wait, I know two you should be extra careful with," Blueberry said, "They're the Wildboys and the Queen. One is a gang of wildmen and the other rules the entire place."

"That's all I needed, thanks for the help."

"No problem."

The rest of the Yard Jungle was easy to get through. Pixies with dragonfly wings made wasp-paper homes on elephant ear leaves. Harpies played experimental rock on tree stumps, using stink bugs as guitar picks. They minded their business and I did the same.

Then I got to the Root Maze. It started at a sheer drop. Massive root serpents twisted in and around each other. Fog hid how far of a drop it was to the bottom.

Wet moss squelched under my shoes. A low rumble came from every direction. Exotic birds cried out haunting tunes. The path was long and continuous, the mist giving away no signs of a future destination. Just when I felt like I was getting close to the end, I heard a new sound amongst all the other ones.

I froze, listening for where it was coming from. A silhouette appeared from the fog. Then more appeared from all around. They slid down other roots like cats and landed onto mine. The shadows surrounded me.

The shadow in front of me showed itself. He had a short snout resembling a strange melding between bear, wolf, and human. His brown fur coat made his leather jacket and cap puff out. He chewed on a toothpick with his long canines.

"You chose a bad time to be walking through our territory," he said.

"Would there have been a better one?" I asked.

"Before the last stranger shot a few of my boys up," he said.

More of the shadows left the fog, revealing monsters the same as the one before me. A bunch of them wore bloodied bandages and splints.

"Best you get a move on while we're in a more sparing mood," the main one said.

Two of the taller monsters flanked me, holding bronze chains.

I cracked my neck and popped knuckles.

"I'm sorry, I can't do that. I have business I need to attend to," I said.

The main monster's eyes narrowed. He pulled his toothpick and flicked it away.

"Wild Boys, fix his attitude."

Before they could react, I threw an uppercut at one of the monsters flanking me and a jab into the other. I pushed the two monsters out of the way.

The main monster stood in the way while more jumped in to stop me. I knocked them away with the butt of my ax. The steel singed their fur, a common reaction fae have with cold steel. The main monster wasn't so easy. He grabbed the handle of my ax, giving one of his men the chance to get a hold of me.

Holding me in the air, a monster tried to crush me with a bear hug. I threw my head back, smashing it against his soft nose. He groaned in pain, releasing me from the grapple. I had no time to recover as one of the monsters tackled me off the root.

We fell for a few seconds. Mist whipped at our eyes before we ended up totally submerged in water. Paradoxically, when I swam up I suddenly had footing that wasn't there before. Knee deep in water, I stood gasping for air.

That was interrupted when the same monster who tackled me tried to charge me. I slipped behind him, wrapped my arms over him, and placed him in a suplex. Throwing his head into the water, I rolled away while he recovered. I pulled my gun and aimed it at him. He froze and raised his hands in the air. Soon the rest of the monsters arrived and surrounded me.

They were ready to close in on me before the head one halted them with a wave of his hand. The monsters paused, allowing their leader to speak.

"That gun… you don't happen to be a Whitlock?" he said.

"Depends on what comes next if I answer," I said.

The leader walked up to me. I lowered my gun. He grinned and wrapped me in a less violent bear hug.

"And here I thought I wouldn't see another Whitlock in a few more decades. I should have known by how hard you were fighting," he said. "Name's Bear. What's got you in our neck of the woods?"

"Bit of a long story, but I'm trying to stop this guy from getting something," I strained through the hug.

"Man, we gotta tell the Queen about you being here. She's gonna freak," Bear said.

"Can that wait? It's a bit of an emergency," I said.

"Oh." Bear let me down. "You can go on ahead while we bring her the news. Just go a bit longer and there'll be a root that'll bring you up to where you were going before."

"Thank you!"

I started running, knowing I lost a lot of time with all that happened.

"Watch out for the flamingos when you get there!" Bear warned.

I had no idea what he meant, but I said yeah anyways.

# CHAPTER 28

Bordering between the Lotus Fields and the Root Maze was the Vine Lands. It was a wetland, resembling the one below the Root Maze. Trees curved to form arches, obscuring the light which the Yard Jungle took for granted.

Vines hung low. Curtains hid many secrets, one of them being Percival himself. I waded through the water, looking between the vines for anything. The place was too quiet. All I heard was croaking frogs and crickets.

I stopped, hearing the movement of water on my right side. Then I heard a shotgun reload. I jumped out of the way, a grouping of vines shredded by buckshot. Plant sinew flew out, painting everything around it in dark algae green. I bolted, more shots going off behind me. I ducked behind a tree holding my gun for dear life.

"No matter how far I run, you are always right behind me," Percival said, his voice an all-encompassing echo.

I had to plan fast or I was dead. There were five guards left. Two had shotguns while three had tommy guns. All of them could tear through me with a pull of a trigger. My jacket was durable, but I wasn't looking to test its limits.

"Really, this whole back and forth is pointless. This was never your fight to have, Jonathan."

The water rippled around the tree I was hiding behind. It came from both sides, meaning they planned to envelope me. I pushed myself into the tree, squishing into a small nook.

One Tommy gun and one shotgun came around to my side of the tree. They searched around for me, unaware that I had hid right behind them.

I peeked my gun out at the shotgun mobster. I fired three shots, two on the body and one on the head. The mobsters splashed into the ground, alerting the other one. It swung around but was knocked down when I fired three shots into its center of gravity. I leapt out, grabbed the shotgun, and shredded the other mobster while it was down.

I went back to chasing Percival. I pushed through the water, using whatever strength I had to go just a bit faster.

"Your uncle kept a lot of secrets, even from you. You're walking in one of his secrets now, the one he'd burn the world to keep. He killed for this place, all because he thought the world wasn't ready for it. You two are truly nothing alike. You discover while he hides. In another reality, he would have given you the same fate he's rewarded so many others," Percival mocked.

I followed his voice, using his insults to guide me to where he truly was. He couldn't help himself anymore, and I took advantage.

Tracking the sound, I stopped at a wide-reaching veil similar to the hanging branches of a weeping willow. Going under the veil, I was introduced to a whole new area.

Unlike the rest of the Vinelands, this area had a good amount of sunlight. Its quietness was a stark contrast to the busyness from before, the green curtains working as a type of sound insulation. The flamingos Bear spoke about peppered the area, deep in slumber. They had no feathers and a plastic sheen like the plants I saw in the Yard Jungle. Their legs were a single thin wire like a lawn flamingo. Despite their unnatural look, their chests went up and down as they slept. Taking Bear's advice, I stayed quiet.

Percival Maelie was standing a few yards in front of me with his wax guards. He kept quiet till I saw him. Noticing how careful I was with the flamingos, he gestured to his guards. The guards slinged their weapons, pulling out knives instead, and began to trudge towards me.

I pulled out my shotgun. The guards stopped and Percival held his hands up to try to stop me. Instead of shooting them, I aimed for the air instead. The blast rang throughout the wetlands, and all the flamingos' eyes shot open. Spooked, they all flew up into the air.

The three guards pulled their weapons. They delayed firing when one was suddenly impaled by a flamingos' leg.

The flamingos were out to shish kebab us. They rained down on us in a torrent of spearing legs. I ran forward, along with Percival and his guards. One by one the guards were impaled; it was just me and Percival now.

Hitting the other end of the veil, I tackled Percival through it. Turns out there was a waterfall laying just behind it. We tumbled off the edge, making it the second time this night I was free falling with someone else. We didn't fall for long, landing in a shallow body of water.

I got up, taking in the whole new area around me. It was the Lotus Fields. We stood atop the seed head of a lotus plant. It looked to be fifty yards in diameter. Pock marks holding seeds covered the top of it. A stream of water fell from the sky and onto the center of the lotus, filling the top with ankle deep water. Surrounding us were other seed heads as massive as the one we were on. Clouds of iridescent butterflies swarmed around the lotuses, including our own.

Percival picked himself up, looking around the environment. His eyes stopped at me. Rage came off him in waves of heat. He clenched his fist, shaking. With that rage came realization. He had disregarded me since the day we met. Now, in his moment of triumph, I proved how much of a threat I truly was.

"Looks like you saw a ghost," I said.

"It's uncanny," Percival said.

Even after he listed how different I was to my uncle, he couldn't shake off what made us similar. We knew how to stop people like him.

"Let's end this here and now, Jonathan," Percival declared.

I couldn't agree more. I was all out of tools. I had lost my ax in the fall. Ammo or no ammo, my gun was useless against him. I was unarmed and so was Percival. The only way to solve this was with our fists.

We approached each other. Face to face, we brought up our fists. Percival threw the first punch. He was good, better than was expected from someone who never lifted a finger in a fight. His fists carried weight and speed, bruising my body with each hit. As we fought, we also talked.

"What was this even all about, huh? Or are you just a big fan of flowers?" I said.

"You wouldn't begin to understand. All this work and planning was in pursuit of more power," Percival said.

"I don't see the correlation. Life dust, scrounging around for coins on dead secret societies, and now a giant lotus in fairyland? What other steps am I missing in this?" I asked.

Percival and I wrestled to put each other in a grapple.

"You really think that secret society is dead? It's alive and well and has the keys to things you can't possibly imagine."

"Oh I think I can. You're not exactly original," I said.

Percival threw me off and we put ourselves back to fighting stance. He wiped his nose, smearing it with blood.

"You have no scale of what's truly happening. When I'm done with you, I will have carved out a world of my own design," Percival said.

Tasting copper, I said, "Don't call a game till it's over."

I charged Percival, jumped up, and kicked him square in the chest. My shoes dug deep into him, my full weight launching him back and onto the ground. Percival coughed. Body flat in the water.

"You ready to surrender?" I let out.

Percival sat up with a heavy breath. Hate in his eyes, he moved and pulled one of the seeds from the pod. I ran to stop whatever he had planned. He smiled, and bit off a piece of the seed in a loud crunch. I kicked the seed away, but it was too late.

Percival swallowed the piece. Once he did, flakes of him began to fly off him like burning paper.

"What—what is happening? What did you do?" I wheezed.

Percival looked at me, for the first time unsure of himself. "We'll find out together."

He slowly turned to dry embers, joining up with the swarms of butterflies. I stood there confused, unable to tell whether I just won or lost. My arms went limp, and only the waterfalls could be heard.

Interrupting the silence, a voice said, "Now that was one good show."

I swung around to meet the voice. They looked like a woman. She was on the heavier side with a scarlet dress and high heels. Black teardrop-shaped makeup bordered her eyes, with white makeup circling around that. The back part of her hair was long and wild while her front was totally bald. It was an intense orange, making it look like a bonfire was always behind her.

"You look like you've been through the ringer," she said.

Her voice was a microcosm of the entirety of the Faerie Mound. It felt like a nice conversation, a flower field on a clear day.

"You must be the Queen I was told so much about," I said.

"In the flesh." She smiled, then asked, "And you're Jonathan Whitlock?"

"I didn't tell them my full name," I said.

"You didn't need to, I know a lot of things. I just wanted to be told about it. Makes it feel more true."

"Huh, can I ask you something?" I said.

"You certainly can."

"What happened to Percival?"

The Queen sighed. "These seeds carry with them the physical manifestation of calmness. It is highly concentrated and can only be consumed by humans in microscopic doses. He's been taken to a world of complete tranquility. If he ever comes back, he will be a whole other person from the man you knew."

"That's... a bit terrifying."

"That goes for all of nature. It is our responsibility to find peace with that," the Queen said.

"So you wanted to see me, right? Why?" I asked.

"Because… I need to tell you that some things will be changing from now on. You can't close what was opened. Unlike my deal with Kasper, I'm intending for my subjects to move more freely between my kingdom and the surface. It'll be up to you, Jonathan, for Helford to adapt."

"But I—" I couldn't find the energy to argue. I fought so much, and my body was beginning to give out.

"No need to speak now. Just rest, everything will be okay."

The iridescent butterflies flew around me in a cyclone. My eyes drifted closed. When I opened them again, I was on the basement floor. Tomas was holding onto me while Charles and Matilda looked over me for any injuries.

"Oh my god, are you okay?" Tomas said.

"I'm alive and that's what matters," I said back.

It felt like a dream. My body struggled to move through the pain and exhaustion.

"You scared the crap out of me," Tomas said.

"I scared myself too, honestly," I said.

"I'm glad you're back," Tomas smiled.

I stayed quiet. I wanted the moment to last just a bit longer. We won, and I couldn't be happier.

# CHAPTER 29

The Queen was right. As soon as the sun got back up, things started to change. Our house was wrecked, and the news was awash with complaints about new creatures causing damage.

The first thing we needed to solve was the cops. They were still out for us, and a squad of deputies were surrounding our house by the time we woke up. We spent a few days in jail, but with Charles's help, we got the evidence to get us out. As it turns out, Trellis set up a makeshift camera system in the factory. All that sweet exonerating footage was left in the laptop the dolls used for text to speech. It was found at the factory, abandoned by the last doll. She's still out there, but that was a future thing to worry about.

Using the cure Percival gave me, we cured everyone that was affected by Trellis's curse. Everyone celebrated afterwards, happy that this tragedy was averted. Harriet Maelie made that day a town-wide holiday called Hush Giving. It's a bit macabre to name a holiday after a guy that got killed in the process of that holiday, but that guy also tried to kill me, so I wasn't too upset.

I talked to Harriet about what happened to her brother. It took a while, since there was a lot to explain. She seemed sad but wasn't devastated.

When I asked her why, she said, "With how he left, to my family and my father especially, he'd been dead to us for over five years."

I knew the Maelie's evil didn't start at Percival, but even that made my hairs stand up. Harriet's mourning period had long since passed. The more I learned about her family, the more context I had for our previous interactions. It can't justify her actions, only give explanations for those acts. Hard to be a light in the darkness when taught to be the exact opposite. She needed a Tomas from the moment she left the womb.

The big stuff was out of order. Charles went ahead and went on his way.

Helping him load his luggage at the motel, I asked him "What are you planning to do next?"

"Don't know, but the road always answers eventually," Charles said.

"It just bums me out. I feel like I still have so much to learn from you," I said.

"Think about it like this: I'm leaving because I know this place is in good hands."

"That helps, it just doesn't get rid of all the worries I have," I said.

Closing his trunk, Charles said, "If you didn't feel that I'd be scared for you."

"Yeah," I nodded.

"Oh, and by the way."

Charles tossed something to me. It was the wood cylinder, the one he came all this way to get.

Before I had a chance to ask why, he said, "Your house's sigils are stronger than anything else I've encountered. It's safer with you than it is with me."

Charles got in his car, starting it up with a good twist of the keys. "You got this, Jonathan. You're good people, and that's the best quality to have in this world. And hey, if you're on the way, I'll visit and say hi. Take care."

Charles drove off to the open road. There wasn't a question in my mind that he'd be fine wherever he went. I'm just shocked he felt the same way about me.

The final part was fixing the wrecked roof. We boarded it up best we could, cleaning off the moss and dirt the fae had thrown around. Done with the roof, Tomas and I sat together and watched the sun set.

"It's so beautiful," Tomas said.

"It really is. If it wasn't freezing, I'd be up here all night."

I felt an aching inside as we watched, an anxiety that made my lungs twist.

Noticing I was bothered, Tomas asked, "What's wrong?"

"I don't know, I feel scared and worried. Everything's going to change now, and I don't know how to feel about it. Will it be good? Will it be bad? All I know is that it's going to be a problem soon."

The wind picked up, chilling the anxious heat built up in my head. Tomas wrapped his hand around mine.

"That's true. It won't be easy, but I don't think it'll be terrible either," Tomas said.

"Why?"

"Because we'll deal with it together." Tomas smiled through red cheeks.

So much happened through this one year. We fought a monster, got a daughter, partied till we saw god, and met the coolest guy in the world. All of that and more happened. Something like that could overwhelm anyone. Yet, even after all of that, I knew we'd be okay in the end.